# ADOPT A VAMPIRE

A Ross Young and Unholy Trifecta Crossover

# AJ Sherwood

This book is a work of fiction, so please treat it like a work of fiction. Seriously. References to real people, dead people, good guys, bad guys, stupid politicians, companies, restaurants, events, products, locations, pop culture references, or wacky historical events are intended to provide a sense of authenticity and are used fictitiously. Or because I wanted it in the story. Characters, names, story, location, dialogue, weird humor, and strange incidents all come from the author's very fertile imagination and are not to be construed as real. No, I don't believe in killing off main characters. Villains are a totally different story.

ADOPT A VAMPIRE - A Ross Young & Unholy Trifecta Crossover

# 1

When people got out of work late, they usually focused on getting home, what to have for a quick dinner, and how fast they could get into comfy sweats. I wasn't any different, although my dinner options were extremely limited thanks to my diet. I hated diets. I especially hated them when they didn't come with an option tag. At least it was Thursday, so I only had to survive one more day of work this week before I could become a couch potato.

My mind focused on my (lack of) dinner plans, I didn't immediately notice the two guys across the street from my downtown office building. I probably wouldn't have noticed them at all, but since the change six years ago, my senses were now a lot keener than the average human's. When the dry Arizona breeze swept my direction, it brought their scent with it, and I froze, keys in hand, halfway reaching for the car door.

What...was that? It smelled like fur and human and iron-rich blood.

They'd caught some hint of me, too, as they were standing very still and watching me with unnatural focus. I swallowed hard and stared back, not sure what to make of this. They were the first supernatural beings I'd seen in six years, and I had no experience whatsoever with weres. At least, judging from the smell, I assumed them to be a were-something. Werewolves, werepanthers—something warm-blooded and furry.

Oh boy. What should I do, here? I'd chosen Arizona on purpose, Flagstaff in particular, as I hadn't wanted to get involved with the supernatural world. The one brush I'd had with it six years ago had done enough damage physically and mentally, so I didn't really want to mix with it again. I'd lived here peacefully for six years without any run-ins, so I didn't know how to take the appearance of these two. Were they just passing through?

As if to answer my question, they looked either direction, then crossed the somewhat busy street, moving a touch faster than a human could manage at a speed walk, only slowing when they reached the sidewalk on my side. I turned to track them, dropping my briefcase and keys on the hood of my car to free up my hands. I had no idea if my weakened state could compete with two weres at full strength. Somehow, I doubted it. I wasn't exactly in peak physical condition these days.

Stopping five feet away, the taller one with two-toned hair informed me flatly, "This is our territory. You can tell Oscar to keep to his own land."

Despite fear causing my heart to beat a staccato against my ribs, I cocked my head. Interesting. Had he mistaken me for someone else? "I'm sorry...who?"

They blinked at me.

I stared back. Did I need to run for my life or...?

"Oscar," the other one said, his dark brows drawing together as if he wasn't sure whether to be confused or angry I was pulling his leg. "You know."

"Ah, no. Really don't," I assured him sincerely. I assumed Oscar was another vampire they knew, maybe someone powerful? I knew zilch about vampire politics and society, so I could only hazard a guess. "I'm not affiliated with any group or family or whatever you call them. Are you two living here? In Flagstaff, I mean."

They stared at me some more.

I stared back, not sure what they'd found so discombobulating. Was it my question of where they lived? I mean, it was a common question with humans, but maybe it was taboo in the supernatural world?

"You're a vampire," Two Tone said slowly, head canting in obvious confusion, "and you don't know who Oscar is."

I gave him my best disarming smile, the one I gave little old ladies. See? I'm harmless, so please do not squish me. "Yeah, sorry, no idea. I take it me being here is some sort of territorial no-no?"

The shorter one shifted forward as I spoke, and his slender frame displayed a more relaxed stance now, his gaze blatantly sizing me up. I knew what I looked like to him— dark hair, pale skin, painfully thin body that even my nice navy suit couldn't disguise. I wasn't the amazingly beautiful vampire from the movies and books, just an average guy who didn't look like Frankenstein's monster. Obviously, I wasn't egging for a fight or accustomed to them. He didn't look hostile, just thoughtful, which made my own guard lower. Maybe not all supernaturals were scary assholes? "It would be, if you were one of Oscar's. So if you're not his, which clan do you belong to?"

Yeah, I was not about to just hand out my life story without some information in return, but these two weren't looking quite as lethal as before, their metaphorical hackles subsiding a little, so I chose to take a risk. It was either that, or waste my one chance to learn how to survive in this new world, 'cause clearly I was sucking at it. So yea, maybe a little conversation here wouldn't hurt anything. "Tell you what, let's just do full introductions all around, shall we? I'm Jesse, and you are?"

"Cesar," the man with two-toned hair responded with a respectful look in his eye, as if he appreciated the gesture of civility. "This is my cousin, Luis. We're from Walker Pack."

"Nice to meet you," I greeted and hoped that stayed true. "To answer, I'm not from a, uh, group. I've only met one other vampire, the one who turned me, and I haven't seen him in six years."

They slowly blinked, then looked at each other like I'd announced the moon really was made of cheese. It lasted only a second before Cesar looked me over from head to toe again, and this time his expression turned puzzled with concern. "You're not a rogue."

That much, at least, I knew something about. "No."

"The vamp who turned you, he was?"

"Yeah. It's how I know what you mean." I shrugged, not having anything else to say without a lot of swearing being involved. The vampire who'd turned me had never outright said he was a rogue, but the way he'd appeared and then disappeared from my life had pretty much connected the dots. "But how can you tell?"

"You're not well fed," Cesar answered bluntly, and he closed the rest of the distance between us, standing in a more conversational range. "Listen, Jesse. This is not a good position for you to be in. We've got three groups edging in on this territory, and one of them's a vampire clan. If you don't align with Oscar's people pretty quickly, someone might mistake you as a rogue, and they'll tear your head off before you can get a hello out. We only hesitated because you weren't doing anything hostile, and we didn't want to start trouble."

Hence they'd tried warning me off first. Got it. "I don't like the idea of just waltzing up to their territory and introducing myself. For one thing, I don't even know where they are." Not to mention they might not exactly be the friendly type.

"Yeah, that's not a good idea," he said, scratching the scruff on his chin. "Tell you what. Let me call my alpha, see if we can get you under our protection until we can reach Oscar. I don't want you to be accidentally killed and them getting in a huff about a vampire dying on our turf."

I could see how that would start a war, even if I wasn't one of theirs. Still... "Look, just so we're clear, I don't want to actually be part of any vampire cult or what have you. It's not my idea of a good time, having someone be master over me. I only want to meet them, ask a few questions."

They gave me the "he's strange" look again. I got that look a lot, so it didn't really phase me anymore.

"Jesse"—Luis couldn't be much older than me, but still

he spoke as if trying to explain something to a child—"you really can't afford to be out here on your own. I know you've managed for a while, so you think you can keep going, but we've got some pretty heavy hitters moving in. It's a miracle you haven't been caught between two sides already. And really? You're too weak to survive the fallout if you did. You look like I can break you over my knee."

Ruefully, I had to admit he had a point. According to movies and lore, vampires were supposed to be ridiculously strong, and the first year after turning, I was. I could bench press five hundred pounds and do ridiculous leaps and feats of strength normally reserved for Olympic athletes. After that, though, I'd been in a steady decline. I'd tried to offset it by eating everything I could think of to stay healthy, but I'd only suffered excruciating stomach pain for my attempts. Seemed the stories had one thing right—a vampire fed best fresh from a human.

And I refused to.

I paused, thinking hard and fast. Should I go along with this? They had good points, and I didn't like the idea of being caught in a clash of supernaturals who would certainly be stronger than me. Still, I'd avoided trouble for six years. I could always find a new job and move. It wasn't like I had vital reasons for staying in Arizona.

Then again, would it hurt to at least meet their alpha? Learn more about werewolves and the supernatural world? Really, I couldn't avoid future trouble without more information than I currently had. Frankly, right now I knew basically nada. "All right. I at least would like to talk to him."

Relieved, Cesar instantly fished his cell out of his pocket and speed-dialed someone. They picked up on the third ring, and I could clearly hear both sides of the conversation from where I stood. "Barrett, its Cesar. We have an interesting problem. There's a vamp living here in Flagstaff, but he's not one of Oscar's."

"*Rogue?*" a smooth tenor voice demanded from the other side.

"No way he is. He's actually quite polite, introduced himself and everything." Cesar shot me a grin. "Says he was turned six years ago by a rogue, and we're the first supernaturals he's seen since."

*"Shit. Poor kid."*

I rolled my eyes a little at his assumption. At thirty-three, I couldn't be considered a kid by anyone's standards.

"Look, Barrett, he's…not in good shape. I don't think he'll survive much longer out here. Can we bring him in until we tell Oscar about him?"

*"An abandoned vampire out on his own for six years? Of course he's not in good shape. Shit, just by being loose, he can start a war without meaning to. Yeah, bring him in—"*

Now I balked. "Wait, wait! You want me to go stay in werewolf territory?"

I got "duh" looks from two people and probably a third, not that I could see through the phone screen.

I glared right back at them. "You seriously expect me to take the word of three people I've barely met and follow you home? Honey bunches of nope, that is not happening."

"Jesse," Luis said, trying to reason with me in that slightly condescending tone parents used for unreasonable kids, "you really can't stay out here. You would be much safer at home with us—"

"It's like that T-shirt," I grumbled rhetorically to the mild evening air. "You have to show me the candy first, then I get into the van. I'm not stupid."

From the alpha on the line, there was a cough that sounded suspiciously like a laugh. Well, at least he saw where I was coming from.

"I don't know you," I told them both bluntly, crossing my arms. "I only have your word things are going to get crazy."

*"Cesar,"* the alpha started, *"he does have a point, and he's right to be wary. Where are you three?"*

"Downtown, near the courthouse."

*"All right. Ask him if he's comfortable meeting me at Sweet Aroma Café."*

The café was literally a block down and one of the few places I could order coconut water straight and not get weird looks from the staff. "That's fine."

He'd obviously heard me as he said, *"Give me twenty minutes."*

Cesar hung up and pocketed the phone, giving me a sideways look. "Don't we need to feed you first?"

I stretched my mouth out in a simulacrum of a grin. "Don't worry. I don't snack on people."

Barrett the Alpha looked like a model. He had a lean build, and while not the bulky type, he clearly possessed a sculpted physique. Even while sitting down, his exposed forearms displayed a ripple of muscle beneath his deep bronze skin, and he radiated authority to the point of being nearly overpowering. Damn, if strength determined the alpha in a werewolf pack, then he was very obviously the guaranteed winner.

His black hair had been cut in a short buzz on the sides, with slightly more length on top. I wanted to put him in his forties, just from the fine lines around his eyes and mouth and the general air of maturity about him, but I had no idea if my guess was accurate. Did werewolves age slower than humans?

I'd arrived at the outdoor table where the three weres sat amidst my assessment and slowly sank into the only available seat. Since I'd been warily watching the alpha now sitting across from me, it was hard to miss his dark brown eyes taking me in and the brief flash of a frown before his expression turned into something more professional. "I'm Barrett Walker. You've already met Luis and Cesar."

"Jesse Hunt," I said, offering a hand. He hesitated a second, surprised at the gesture, then slowly took it, his calloused hand folding over mine. I could feel the strength behind his grip. I had no idea what he actually did for a living, but it must have required that strength, as dust and mortar of some sort were smudged in various places. Stonemason, maybe? He smelled of stone, powder, sweat, and sunshine, a not unpleasant concoction.

"Well, Jesse, I have to say I didn't expect to casually sit down to dine with a vampire when I got up this morning." He gave me a quick smile, a lopsided expression that relayed dry humor. "Tell me, how long have you been in Flagstaff?"

"About six years," I admitted. "I tried to stay where I was before...well, before." I didn't know how to say this with people all around us, so I lowered my voice a smidge to avoid being overheard. "But it didn't work out well. I wasn't at work for a few days, and when I went back, too many people caught on to me acting different, more withdrawn, and thought I was on drugs. I eventually had to move, and my maker had briefly mentioned that most supernats didn't like to live in the desert, so I came to Arizona. It's worked out pretty well the past six years."

"We're expanding territory because we've basically overpopulated the other favorite places to live," Barrett admitted openly. "And not everyone dislikes the desert. In this case, it works out well for your people, and for mine, so long as we have large empty places to run around. We've got a group of witches who are budging in here, and it's causing some conflict because we didn't expect them. Honestly, they're the ones I'm worried about the most where you're concerned. They've got some hotheads."

I grimaced. He didn't have to tell me that. It was a group of witches that led to me being turned in the first place. "How many?"

He caught my uneasy reaction but didn't comment. "We can't get a fixed number on them, which is part of the problem. They stuck to the southwest part of town for the first few months, but now they're flexing and pushing, and we see them up here sometimes too." He adjusted his forearms against the tabletop, making the glass shift in its metal frame. "Oscar's people aren't settled yet, not really, so they're still trying out areas and figuring out which spots they're going to fight to keep. We've been here longest, as we moved in eight months ago."

"So this is all very new." I sat back, frowning. That did make sense. No wonder I hadn't seen anyone before now, if they'd started on the outskirts of town and were feeling their way toward the center. I lived and worked downtown, so of course I hadn't been in anyone's sight yet, but that changed as of today. If I had run across another vampire, or one of those witches, would I have ended up at this outdoor table in front of the café? Or would I be fighting for my life right now?

Probably the latter.

"Jesse, I have to ask some questions." Barrett looked at me carefully, as if trying to gauge my reaction.

"I've got some too," I admitted steadily. A little game of quid pro quo seemed appropriate for this setting. "Since you've been explaining a lot, you start."

He very obviously phrased the question in his head before speaking it. "How are you surviving?"

A very wise question, if he still considered bringing me into his territory a good idea. "Coconut water."

Barrett winced.

I felt defensive for some reason and snipped at him, "What was I supposed to do? I'm not feeding from people. Coconut water is very similar to blood. More acidic and without all the same nutrients, sure, but close enough to keep me alive. I tried eating raw steak and other foods, to offset things, but for some reason my system didn't like it. So now I'm on a permanent liquid diet."

"Damn," Cesar muttered to himself, sitting on Barrett's right side. "No wonder you're stick-thin."

I glared at him mutinously. I wasn't on this extreme diet because I wanted to be. Human food literally did nothing for me. It tasted fine, I could eat and enjoy it, but my body always rebelled soon after, which led to hours in pain and still feeling weak. I could eat all day and starve. The coconut water was the only thing I'd found I could subsist on. "My turn for a question, I think. You said Oscar is new to the area. What's he like?"

"Not much known about him," Barrett admitted, still watching me with open pity. "He's not actually a clan master, you understand, but a lieutenant for one. Oscar's here with about twenty others, and I think they're just placeholders more than anything else. A way for his master to expand territory while it's still open to be claimed. I've met Oscar exactly twice, and he's amiable enough if you're polite and open to negotiation. Or at least, he didn't act like a complete asshole. Don't get me wrong, he's still a jerk, but all vampires are jerks to weres. It's a superiority thing, but you likely won't have an issue with him. His master is Nash, one of the oldest vamps, and he's up in Vancouver."

This surprised me, but I didn't know why. Vancouver, as a city, wasn't that old. I guess I expected him to say an older place, like Boston or something. "So this is more like a branch office."

"Something like that, yeah. Look, I know you're not keen on mixing with vamps, the only time you did it led to this"—he gave me a general wave of the hand to indicate all my vampiricalness—"but not all of them are bad. I can at least vouch for Oscar. He isn't a bad guy. If we explain the situation to him, at the very least he'll ensure you're within the clan's boundaries and aren't hassled."

"Yeah, but at what cost?" I stared Barrett down as he faltered. "Look, I'm not used to having someone to answer to. I'm not saying I want to go hog wild, here, but I have a feeling joining a vampire group is like joining the army. Forever. Not my cup of tea."

"It's more like being part of a large community," Luis said, correcting me. He leaned back in his chair, comfortably sitting to keep us both in view as he talked. "Only the top vamp leaders will order you around, and they rarely do this. I mean, Nash's clan—clan is the official term for vampires—

is huge, almost a thousand people. There's no way he has time to order every single person around."

Said like that, it did ease my fears. Clan, huh? He said it wasn't like the military, but I wondered if it might be something more like a family? I hadn't had one of those in a long time and my heart ached at the thought of getting to have one again. It hadn't been fun living on my own for a long stretch of time, and the novelty wore off in the first six months. I still didn't know these people, so I didn't have any intention of just jumping into matters, but I didn't mind at least meeting them. If nothing else, I had a lot of questions I wanted answered about being a vampire. "I guess it doesn't hurt to at least talk to them."

"I really, really don't want anyone to mistake you as a rogue," Barrett informed me with transparent sincerity. "It will cause all sorts of issues for us, and you seem like a nice guy. It'll be a pity to see you hurt. Let's at least notify Oscar you're here so mistakes won't be made, yeah? And come home with me for the evening, stay with us until someone from the clan can come meet you. It'll be a lot safer, and I won't have a nervous breakdown that way." Barrett shot me a cheeky grin before adding, "And before you protest, just know I'm Cuban, and we love hosting people. Not to mention most of my pack treats my house like their own, anyway. I promise, you won't be a burden, and I can guarantee my people will treat you well."

Strangely, I believed him. Over the course of our conversation, my guard had slipped, and I didn't fear for my safety at all. Which...uh, why?

Instincts, I'm asking a question, here. Would love a response, please and thank you. This man could break me like a toothpick.

Of course, part of me still hesitated because going home with three relative strangers seemed like a poor life decision, but truthfully, they could force me into a car if they wanted to. Barrett alone could do so with one arm. I also got this sincere vibe from him, or maybe it was his body language. He'd been very open with me, and it made me want to respond in kind. I just didn't think I was in danger with him. Call me crazy, but my instincts insisted I was safe as houses. He'd politely asked, he had good reasons, and it wouldn't kill me to spend a few hours at his house cooling my heels. "If we don't get an answer by nine, I'll return to my place. I'm right off this square, so it's not like I'm openly in someone else's territory, right?"

"Just ours," he assured me with a grin. "And yeah, that's fine. But still, I think Oscar will answer pretty quickly. I'll be surprised if this takes more than two hours to resolve."

"Come home and let us feed you, yeah?" Cesar invited with a waggle of his brows. "I'll let you snack on me."

I frowned at him. "No, thank you."

Not expecting my response, he pulled his head back. "Why not? Seriously, you're a vamp, what do you have against blood?"

"You smell like wet dog," I retorted. "No way."

Barrett threw his head back and howled a laugh.

# 2

Let me tell you something, being in a werewolves' den was a whole different experience. Barrett's house sat in the middle of a quaint neighborhood, a two-story stucco with amazing rock work around it. My guess of Barrett being a stonemason by trade was obviously dead-on. But on the other hand, these people had absolutely no concept of personal space. I barely got through the front door when I found this out the hard way.

Four very cute furballs tumbled right into my shins. Apparently, when the kids were home, they chose to romp around in puppy form—puppy form, naturally, being about the size of a full-grown dog. Three layers of sandstone-colored fur made them soft and round looking, and I couldn't for the life of me think of them as something dangerous. They tumbled right into my legs then paused at my feet, looking up at me curiously.

"Will you four quit," Barrett growled at them, sounding exactly like an exasperated yet doting uncle. "We have a guest; you shouldn't be bowling him over."

One of them yipped something, the tone lilting up like a question.

"Yes, he's a vampire. Fortunately a nice vampire. Shoo. We have things to talk about."

Being kids, only two of them listened and immediately went to another room; the third shuffled backward but stayed, curiosity making the child linger, and the fourth lifted their head to nose at my wrist, inhaling deeply. I let them do so, watching sharply in return. I'd grown up around dogs—my parents raised collies most of my childhood—so I knew something about canine behavior. But how much of my knowledge applied to someone who had the instincts of a dog but the intelligence of a human?

"Grace," Barrett warned in a low tone. "Quit."

"She's all right," I assured him, meaning it. "She's just curious. I probably don't smell like any other vampire she's seen, what with my odd diet."

Barrett gave me an odd look. "True enough. You don't. You're pretty comfortable being surrounded by the furballs."

"Grew up with collies," I explained with a shrug. "They're about the same size and also have no concept of personal space. Kinda reminds me of my childhood."

Grace whined in protest.

"Well, if you don't want me to treat you like a dog," I responded archly, "then don't act like one."

Her ears went flat as she whined again. Barrett laughed, grinning down at her. "He's got you there. Come on through, Jesse. Dining room is probably the best place to park it, as it's usually mostly clear until the dinner rush starts. It's a whole thing, so brace yourself."

I followed him through the entrance and shortly saw what he meant. We quickly came across a lively scene in the living room, where two huge sectionals and every part of the room were covered with either people lounging or puppies demanding attention. I got more than one curious look as we walked past. A few looked borderline alarmed and conversation tapered off, but Barrett simply dismissed their concern with a flippant wave of his hand. Which, wow, that was some obvious trust right there because most turned back to whatever activities they'd been engaged in and the noise level once again rose, with only a few intrigued stares lingering.

We left the hardwood for tile as we crossed into the dining room. There was a vibrant landscape up on the far wall, but no other decorations. Probably because there wasn't room for more if the pack frequently gathered here. The room held a massive dining room table, easily able to sit fifteen people, chairs given just enough room on all sides to be pulled back. I saw more people in the open-concept kitchen taking me in curiously, whom Barrett just waved away again. I took note of a set of French doors leading to the backyard, where I could see even *more* people loitering around the big swimming pool or under the patio awning, with several others dancing in the sparse grass to a quick and lively tempo. Good grief, this was the mostly clear he'd mentioned? Just how many people were in this house? Forty? Fifty?

Something of disbelief must have shown on my face. As we sat down near the head of the dining table, Barrett remarked, "It's pretty busy here most days up until bedtime. Then people actually clear out to their own homes. Being alpha means I'm rarely ever alone, but I don't mind it. I'd rather have them close. We have strong family values, and dinner especially is a large affair around here."

Duly noted, but I found myself drawn to the warm, inviting ambiance in this house. Even a complete stranger like myself wasn't uncomfortable here. It also smelled strongly of cumin and citrus, a testament to the hearty meal being prepared for all to enjoy. Compared to the cold silence of my apartment, it was overwhelming, but I envied it a little, too. "If you have family, enjoy them."

He nodded in agreement, but something in his eyes and how he looked at me suggested he found my comment interesting. Or perhaps troubling. "I've got some coconut water in the fridge. You want one to sip on while I make the phone call to Oscar?"

My stomach gurgled happily at the idea. Or maybe that was its lodged complaint of neglect, hard to tell. "Please, if you don't mind."

"I've got it," a slender woman said to Barrett, already sailing past the table. "Although I don't think a drink from the fridge is what our guest needs. Surely someone wouldn't mind feeding him."

I held up a hand, stopping this idea before it got off the ground. "Thank you, but no."

"Our guest is against feeding from people," Barrett informed her before turning back to me. "The saucy brunette is my lieutenant, Marissa. She's a nutritionist as well, so maybe she'll know of something else you can have that will get some meat back on your bones."

I perked up with interest, regarding her more closely as she weaved amongst people preparing food. She wore black slacks and a dressy purple blouse, something office appropriate, hair done up in a simple twist at the back of her head. A pretty woman, and if I swung that way, I might have flirted just because. "That would be good."

"This is Jesse Hunt." Barrett completed the introduction with a wave at me, and I saw several other people's ears perk up, no doubt intrigued by the information. "He was turned by a rogue about six years ago. We're the first supernaturals he's seen since."

Marissa stopped mid-motion in reaching for the fridge door. "How in the world did you manage that?"

"No one was here then," I responded, avoiding the full history and explanation. I just didn't feel like giving it for a second time today. "It was actually easy."

With a sharp look at me—I had a feeling she hadn't bought my story—she rummaged through the fridge before pulling something out. I saw the blue and white label and smiled in relief. It would help my hunger a smidge.

As she bustled about, occasionally pausing to let someone pass, Barrett pulled his phone out and dialed a number. It rang a few times before it clicked on and he got an answer.

"*Well, Alpha Barrett, this is an unexpected call. Please do inform me that there is no trouble brewing.*"

I blinked at the distinct British accent.

"Not as such," Barrett denied calmly, keeping his eyes on me as he spoke, "but it has the potential for it. Are you aware you have a lone vampire living in this area?"

"*A rogue?*" Oscar demanded sharply.

"No, he's not that. He's actually quite polite and law abiding. Came up and introduced himself and everything." Barrett gave me a teasing wink. "He tells me he was turned by a rogue vampire six years ago, and we're the first supernaturals he's seen since."

*"That...is a very strange story."*

"You'd believe it more readily if you could see him. He's not exactly well. Oscar, I have him at my house, and I'd really prefer we continue this conversation with you present. I think there's a lot you'll want to ask him, I know he has lots of questions for you, and I want this cleared up before anyone mistakes him as a rogue and attacks him. That kind of thing will lead to all sorts of trouble."

*"I quite agree, but I'm not currently in a position where I can just drop in for tea. I'm outside of Flagstaff at the moment and don't anticipate I'll return before late tomorrow. In the meantime, shall I send someone to meet with you and get the particulars? At the very least, I'd like to have one of my own people see him and report to me."*

Barrett lifted an eyebrow, silently asking me if I was all right with this. I didn't mind and nodded in encouragement. The sooner we got this over with, the better.

"That's fine."

*"Then, expect someone within the hour."*

Barrett recited the address to his house before he ended the call and laid his phone on the table. About that point, Marissa finally wrestled herself free from the kitchen crowd and deposited two bottles of coconut water in front of me. I didn't fall on them like a ravenous animal, although it was a near thing. As much as I had solid control when it came to blood, being around this many werewolves was giving me some issues. They had more iron-rich blood than a human—I could smell the difference, and it made my mouth water. Even with both drinks in my system, I might have to step outside at some point to avoid...that. At this rate, my craving for blood just might send me over the edge.

I gave Marissa a smile. "Thanks."

"You're welcome," she said, coming around to sit on my other side. Her blue eyes made no secret of the way she studied me as I sipped my drink. "Mr. Hunt—"

"Whoa. Jesse, please," I requested.

"Jesse, then. I do understand why you'd avoid feeding from someone, but we're willing to shed a little blood for you. There's really no reason to make do with something as paltry as coconut water."

I shook my head before she could trot all of that out. "I can't. I've never once fed on human blood."

Barrett inhaled sharply, startled.

"I can't get the taste in my mouth," I told her firmly, even as part of me wistfully dreamed about doing just that. "Today, you're willing to help me out. Tomorrow, I'll be back to this same diet. My willpower isn't *that* good, to know what I'm missing and still refrain. Easier to not know."

A pinched expression drew her face inward as she looked me over from head to toe again. She didn't have to say it out loud because we were all thinking it: I was starving. Literally, slowly starving to death. Part of the reason why I wanted to talk to Oscar was to learn how vampires legally and ethically fed themselves. The rogue vamp hadn't taught me anything beyond surviving. He'd taught me precious little, in fact. If I could just learn their secret, my life would be much better for it.

If not, well...I didn't know how much longer I'd live.

I focused on my drink, gulping down a mouthful and sighing in pleasure. It did taste good, so I at least had that going for me.

"Tell me, Jesse. What do you do for a living?" Barrett inquired.

"Lawyer," I answered carefully around my mouthful. "I focus on real estate and tax law."

"The boring stuff."

"The boring and lucrative stuff," I agreed ruefully. "I hadn't planned it when I'd gone through college, but I interned at a law firm that mostly handled inheritance cases and real estate, and then I was offered a job after graduating. I got sucked into it, I guess. Made it easy when it came time to move, as everyone needs someone with my skill set."

"Especially with parts of the West's real estate market booming," Barrett remarked, relaxing back into his chair. "I run a construction business, and it's part of the reason why we moved here. Business is good, very good, as I'm sure you're aware."

"Yeah, the common complaint around Flagstaff at the moment is not having enough good skilled labor. I bet your company is in high demand. Do you do handyman work or renovations?"

"Sure, it's all part of the trade. Why?"

"People buying up properties constantly ask who I'd recommend to do some work. Give me a stack of business cards, and I'll hand them out."

Barrett gave me a surprised, delighted smile. "Sure. I'll get you some before you leave."

"Where were you before this?"

"Northern California, actually. We were running out of business up there, and the packs in Oregon had started to encroach on our territory." Barrett shrugged, as if this wasn't unexpected. "Population boom, at least among the weres. They bought us out, gave us the money and means to move elsewhere. I don't have a large pack, only about two hundred people, so it was easier all around for us to pull up stakes rather than try to fight with them over territory."

"Weres, not vampires?" I asked, drink temporarily forgotten as I focused on getting some answers.

"Vampire clans as a rule don't grow quickly, or experience 'baby booms,'" Marissa explained patiently. "Only rogue vampires irresponsibly turn others into vampires, you see. Established, older vampires have better sense than that, and they're very careful on who they turn. Rogues usually don't give the new vampires any sort of information or training, and the newly turned often go wild as a result and get themselves killed very quickly. You're one of the rare few who's survived the initial rebirth process. I'd say there's less than a hundred vampires on earth who are younger than fifty years old."

I startled at the number, staring at her with wide eyes. "You're kidding. That few?"

"Not many are turned to begin with," she said with a shrug. "And those who are usually don't survive the first year, which is why Oscar reacted so quickly in sending someone to meet you. The younger vampires are better with technology and understand current trends more than the older vampires, so they're a precious commodity. When vampire clans do discover a young vampire, they take them in if at all possible."

That sounded potentially good but also potentially troublesome. I hadn't realized it was so rare for new vampires to be made, but in a way it made sense. Vampires would have overrun the world already and I would have met some over the last few years if the situation were different. "So you're saying I have some bargaining power. I don't necessarily have to throw my lot in with Nash's group."

"Correct. Although from what we know of him, he's not a bad leader. He's one of the more business savvy of the vampire clans, at least." Marissa nudged the second bottle of coconut water closer, a gentle reminder to drink and listen. "You'd do far worse than joining him."

I took her advice with a grain of salt and went back to sipping.

"Oscar will be very excited to hear you're a lawyer," Barrett mused. "You've got the sort of information and training that makes their lives easier."

Yeah, I'd bet. If you constantly had to change identities in order to avoid detection from humans, it meant selling properties, doing creative things with tax history, etcetera. I'd worried about meeting vampires and having any ground to stand on, but apparently I had some bargaining power just because of my education. Good to know.

I chatted some more with Barrett and Marissa, learned a few more things, but the smell got to me eventually. The rich scent of blood was so much stronger from a were, stronger than from any human, and it made my canines ache. I think Barrett realized it first, as he offered to walk with me outside and let dinner settle a little. I gratefully seized the excuse and went with him.

The outside air had the twilight scent of warm stone and baked pavement. I stood on the sidewalk for a moment, looking around the neighborhood properly. It had the cookie-cutter look of most subdivisions, the houses all eerily similar to each other as if stamped from the same mold. Which, in a sense, they had been. I saw differences with some of them, recognized the same handiwork as the landscaping around Barrett's house, and connected the dots. "This entire street belongs to your pack."

"The entire subdivision basically belongs to us," Barrett corrected. "We got a steal on most of it because they were foreclosed houses and in bad condition. Still have three of them that aren't completely done yet, but we're almost there."

I heard a vehicle approaching before I saw it round the corner, coming onto this street. A dark SUV sharply pulled up to the curb near us, half straddling the rocky landscaping. It jerked to a stop before a pale man with close-cropped platinum hair hopped out of the driver's side and came straight for me.

Something about his expression, his attitude, screamed danger. I fell back a step, wary, because I didn't like the way he stalked toward us. Barrett didn't either, as he took a step closer to me, a warning growl in his throat.

The vampire stopped and spared him a glance. "Oscar sent me. I'll handle this."

*Handle?* Excuse you very much, what was that supposed to mean?

In the next second, his pale hand darted out almost faster than I could track, striking as fast as a viper. In my weakened condition, even though I instinctively realized his intentions, I still had trouble jerking out of range.

Something cold and sharp sliced the skin above my collarbone, angling sideways across my neck, and I felt a trail of fire in its brutal wake as I tried to escape. At the exact same moment, Barrett burst into motion, grabbing the hand holding the blade and jerking it roughly back. I heard the sharp snap of a bone giving way, and then the vampire's face contorted as he screamed in pain.

Gasping, I fell back several steps, hand grasping my open wound, instinctively trying to stop the flow of blood. I could feel the hot liquid pouring out against my trembling fingers and groaned in dismay and pain. Dammit, I didn't have enough blood in my system as it was, and this idiot was putting holes in me!

People burst out of the houses on all sides, likely alerted by the scent of blood and the screaming, and more than one person went wolf as they tumbled through the door. It made the already tense atmosphere turn lethal. I desperately tried to keep my feet, to stay alert in case the vampire lunged again, but it was hard to pay attention while choking on my own blood.

Outraged, Blondie held his broken arm defensively against his torso and spat at Barrett, "What the hell do you think you're doing?"

"That's my line," Barrett snapped back, and in that instant, amidst my pain, I saw why he was the alpha. This slender man suddenly gave the impression he was twice his actual size, his tone so firm and unyielding that rocks would have leapt to obey him. "I called Oscar for a peaceful relay of information and a meeting, not for you to go stabbity on someone who is a *guest in my territory.* Are you completely shit for brains?!"

The vampire stupidly bristled instead of apologizing. "I'm well within my rights to—"

"GET OFF MY LAND," Barrett roared, the hair on his body lifting as if he were seconds away from going full wolf. Several other werewolves howled in agreement or snarled in warning, backing up their alpha.

He might have been stupid, but Blondie apparently had survival instincts. Seeing himself surrounded by hostile werewolves on all sides, he paled even further before scrambling for the safety of the SUV. It took seconds for him to start the engine and gun it out of the cul-de-sac.

Danger now gone, I was losing the battle to stay conscious when Marissa was suddenly right there beside me with a towel, which she pressed against the wound while trying to support my swaying body. I hissed but gratefully moved my hand to allow this, as the towel would be much better at staunching the blood than my soaked fingers.

"Shit, this is bad. It nicked the artery," Marissa hissed out. "He damn near tried to take your head off, and you're not in good enough shape for your regenerative powers to quickly take care of this. What the hell was that idiot doing?"

"I don't know, but Oscar's ears will ring from this." Barrett had some assassin eyes going on, visibly livid as he gingerly lifted the towel for a second to get a look. "Dammit. Let's get him inside. Marissa, call Hector."

"Hector won't know how to fix this," Marissa protested.

Hector must be some sort of doctor. I would have put my two cents in, but the blood loss made me dizzy, and my head felt lighter by the second. My knees buckled, too, and I just knew what was going to happen next and tried to gurgle out, "I'm...gonna fain—"

"Shit." Barrett reached out and grabbed me just as blackness took over.

I was on fire, or at least felt like I was. Unable to focus beyond a haze of intense pain, I barely registered the soft and cushiony surface under me, or the sopping wet towel pushed against my aching throat. Unable to even scream, I couldn't focus on anything beyond the burning pain along my frayed nerves. My skin felt like charred kindling, and I was desperately, desperately thirsty. My only relief was a sweet, rich aroma just out of reach, a siren's call to my instincts. If I could just find the source, I'd be free from this utter agony.

Unable to move, lost to thoughts of finding the overpowering aroma, I caught muffled voices nearby, as if I were listening through cotton.

"—too weak! He should have been able to ward that attack off and heal himself before I even got the call," a male voice I didn't recognize said tartly. "I don't know what you expect me to do. For pity's sake, feed the poor man!"

"We *tried*," a voice that sounded like Marissa's snapped from somewhere nearby. "He refuses to feed from people. He says if he does it once, it'll be too hard for him to resist in the future."

"If you don't feed him properly now, he won't have to worry about it, as he'll be *dead* in the very near future," the unknown voice retorted, sounding fed up. "He doesn't even have anything left to bleed! Here, hand me my bag. I'll feed him."

At those words, a modicum of awareness returned, the feeling of dread swift and sharp.

"*No.*" The alpha had spoken, the single word containing a wealth of command and power. "I'll do it. Wrist?"

"That would be the easiest in his condition. And Barrett, I agree you have the best chance of holding him down if he loses control, but he's lost too much blood to be able to feed from just one donor. Let's take this in turns. I'll go next."

A pause, then came a clipped, "Fine."

"N-no," I rasped in denial, panicking even more when I couldn't get my eyes to open. Oh god, no, if they did that, I'd be screwed. I wanted to protest more, to tell them to just let me die—I couldn't live with becoming a monster—but I couldn't push any more words past my mangled throat.

A warm hand carded through my hair, and Barrett's low voice whispered near my ear but sounded far away. "Jesse, you don't deserve to die, and I can't watch you do it. Please, let us help you. I promise you, you won't be alone after this.

You won't have to starve ever again."

What was he saying? What did he mean? I wanted to ask, but once again I couldn't get the words to formulate, succumbing to another wave of pain. Barrett didn't give me the time to ask more questions, anyway. I heard a slicing sound, and then the heady, wonderfully sharp scent of fresh blood overwhelmed my fractured mind.

Just like that, all my willpower flew out the window, and my body gave over to instinct, only seeking sweet relief. I didn't even remember what the word "resist" meant, much less why I should. Something touched my lips, warm and wet, giving me the relief I sought, and I latched onto it greedily. My hands weakly rose, tilting that smooth appendage for a better angle, and I sucked on it with a deep moan of satisfaction, the noise wet and gurgled.

"Well. To no one's surprise, he's still polite about matters even while he's eating," Marissa observed in amusement, her words clearer than before, less muffled. "And here I thought he'd bite in like a starved dog."

"It's not as painful as I thought it would be, either," Barrett informed her thoughtfully. "It's almost...pleasant? As strange as it sounds. It now makes more sense to me why people volunteer to be blood donors."

I felt like they were being rude, talking about me right over my head, but I really couldn't bring myself to care as the scaring pain along my nerves quieted. I lapped at the open wound with heady delight, enjoying the feeling of consuming something that actually filled my stomach for once. The rich taste was nothing short of addictive, and I wanted to drink until I fell into a food coma, but that would be rude and inconsiderate to the man kind enough to feed me. I took two more swallows before I forced myself to stop and pull back. It took a few more moments before I finally found the strength to open my eyes, needing to orient myself.

"No," Barrett ordered firmly, pressing his wrist back against my mouth. "You're not anywhere close to full. Keep going."

With my hands still on his wrist, I had the leverage to push back, barely. He wasn't even using a quarter of his strength, though, I could tell. "I-I don't want to drain you." I had to force the whispered words around a small lump in my throat, but I figured they got the message.

"He's right," Hector—I assumed this middle-aged man standing behind Barrett to be Hector, at least—intervened. "It's safe enough for us to help, Barrett. Let me go next."

As Hector left to fetch a fresh scalpel, I turned my head just enough to catch Barrett's worried eyes and tried for a smile. "Thank you. You're, uh, delicious."

He snorted, then burst out laughing, although it sounded tinged with disbelief. "You're welcome. God, you scared me. I'm glad you're feeling well enough to joke."

"Is it a joke if it's true?" I teased him in a low voice. I really did feel much better. Even with a cut on my throat, I hadn't felt this good in years.

Barrett gave me a relieved smile. "I'll take your word for it. Let's check on your wound before Hector steps in. Does it still hurt?"

"Stings," I admitted, then winced when he gently pulled the towel off. It had dried enough around the edges to make removing it distinctly unpleasant. "How's it look?"

"Wound is closing," he answered in patent relief. "Let Hector and Marissa feed you some, then we'll try cleaning you up."

Hector came around to sit at my bedside, his hip against mine. He was older than Barrett, more stocky in build, kind brown eyes meeting mine. He radiated heat like most of the pack members, and he carefully held a scalpel near his wrist, waiting on my signal. "Pleasure to meet you, Jesse."

"And you, Hector," I responded, still careful to speak slowly, bemused at the situation I found myself in. "I'm glad you're all willing to help, I really am, but I'm not sure if I need you to slit your wrist on my account, too."

"Why don't you listen to the doctor and eat anyway?" he responded acerbically.

Granted, he had more expertise than me. As I fed, it finally struck me that the one thing I'd feared—losing my head when presented with fresh blood—hadn't happened. I'd done it, I'd pulled away without hurting someone or taking too much. Holy shit. Too many vampire movies had made me think I'd lose all control, but really, people didn't lose their minds over food. I mean, I'd never gone insane over delicious curry or ice cream. Turned out feeding as a vampire wasn't much different. The relief washing through me at the realization was so strong I nearly went giddy under the force of it.

Hector fed me for a few minutes, and it intrigued and disturbed me a little to find he tasted different from Barrett. Not bad different, just...different. Why? Then Marissa fed me, and she tasted different too. This was worrisome because if people could taste different, then that meant people could taste bad. Or really, really good. And what happened if I got a particular craving? I couldn't just go around snacking on people on a whim.

As my thoughts swirled, I felt a little stronger with each passing moment. I could only equate it to how a dehydrated man wandering through a desert would feel, how his first sip of water would taste like nectar of the gods, and then every bottle of water he drank after that gave back his body the strength it had lost. I felt so, so much better with every mouthful.

I lost track of time during those feedings. I just knew from the streetlight coming in from the windows that it was now night outside. The wound on my throat had taken longer to close than Hector would have liked, but it eventually did, leaving me with a pale pink line he swore would disappear completely after another day. My dress shirt and jacket had long since been removed, probably because they'd been in the way and drenched in blood, so Marissa had borrowed a shirt from Barrett's closet while the men carefully cleaned me up. Barrett gently lowered the warm pullover on me, and it smelled strongly of sun and the alpha werewolf, a scent I already connected with things like "friendship" and "safety." I basically swam in the material, like a child playing dress up, but I didn't want to complain. It was very comfortable and soft. Only then, with me more or less set to rights, did Barrett sit next to me on the bed.

His bed, I realized belatedly. The mattress and bedding all smelled of him, and the pictures he had up on the walls and the traces of him I could see around the room made it very obvious this was his bedroom. Wow. For some reason, I felt privileged.

"First, Jesse," Barrett started with a very angry expression, "I must apologize. I never once thought you'd be in danger from your own kind. Especially with me telling Oscar you weren't a rogue, I didn't anticipate any trouble. I should have guarded you better."

I held up both hands. "I think you're very much not to blame for this, Barrett. It's clear to me there was either a misunderstanding or that blond idiot acted on his own agenda. Oscar gave no indication over the phone that he thought you were harboring trouble. Unless you think he was just pretending?"

Barrett immediately shook his head, looking rumpled and tired. "No. I meant what I said earlier. You're a valuable resource for any vampire clan, and even without him knowing everything about you like I do, I can't imagine he'd be so hasty in judgment. It's more likely a misunderstanding, but now I can't trust his people with you. I'm going to call him again in a few minutes and tell him what happened, but I want to ask a few things first. Now that you've fed from people, are you still scared of it?"

A reasonable question. I wasn't sure how to answer him, but I tried to put my impressions into words and capture what I now instinctively understood. "Not...as much. I always thought I'd lose control if my teeth ever met skin, and honestly, it's what worried me the most. I didn't want to become a monster. But I was still in complete control of myself while feeding from all of you. The only thing I'm worried about now is finding people willing to be my donor. I'm, uh, not sure how to manage that and keep my identity intact."

He held up a hand, stopping me. "Worry about that part later. So you're all right with feeding from people now? Good. Okay, here's my thought. This is a strange situation, and not everyone will agree with me, but hear me out. First off, everyone in the pack who's met you likes you."

I blinked at him. What?

"Werewolves get a pretty quick impression of someone," he explained, mouth curling up at the edges as if he knew very well what I was thinking, "and it normally doesn't take more than a few seconds for us to decide if we'll like someone or not. I know you're going to become good friends with us. It's just a matter of time. We really don't like the idea of you being out on your own, especially if you can't trust other vampires. I also hate the idea of a man with your willpower and skills going to waste, especially when my pack could use them. You're in the perfect position to help us with the nitty gritty details that come along with keeping our identities hidden. All that said, I don't want to call another vampire clan and give them another shot at taking you in. Why don't you just stay with us instead?"

# 3

I froze, going unnaturally still as only a vampire could. He didn't really mean that, did he? A vampire, living with werewolves? Was this even a thing?

Marissa and Hector both drew in sharp breaths of surprise, so clearly they hadn't expected Barrett's offer either. However, neither protested. They looked at their alpha, first in wonder, then shrewdly, as if they'd caught on to his line of reasoning.

Bully for them, but that didn't mean I got it. "You want me—a vampire—to live with your pack?"

Barrett shrugged like this wasn't the big deal I was making it out to be. "Why not? As I said, I like you. And you'll be a benefit to my pack. Wouldn't you rather stay with us, enjoy having the family and protection that comes along with joining us? Plus, we're super fun. We have big dinners every night, and family game nights once a week, and usually there's a live music night that happens at least once a month so people can cut loose and dance."

I opened my mouth to say, well, something, only to close it again slowly. He had me there. I'd been alone for years and frankly hadn't enjoyed it. It was nerve-racking to be out on my own, and even though I managed, it wouldn't have been my first choice. I just hadn't had an alternative. But now, suddenly, I did. With people I barely knew.

People who'd automatically come to my defense. People who'd fed me while I was starving and on death's door.

I'd yearned for years to have just a single soul I could confide in, and here I was being offered all of that. My heartstrings tugged at the sharp longing that filled me. I yearned for a family again and this...this was something I'd never even dreamed of, being offered to me on a silver platter.

What would it be like, really, living among them? I'd seen how much affection they had for each other, how they instantly pulled together defensively if there was trouble. It hadn't taken more than two hours around them to see this all very clearly. If I was with them, if I was *one of* them...the mental image filled me to bursting. I hadn't felt hope like this in years.

I was not by nature a reckless person, or one given to following their instincts. It prevented me from just jumping in. I went with caution instead. "Barrett. I like the sound of this offer, you've no idea how much, but I don't want us to act impulsively. Maybe let's do this on a trial basis? Take the next six months and decide. Right now, I barely know enough to really make an informed decision."

He nodded, mouth easing up into a smile. "I thought you'd say that. And it's more than fine. Reasonable, really. If in six months, we find a vampire clan who will do right by you, I'll let you go without protest. Sound fair?"

And that was the only way he'd let me go, eh? The thought amused me. I figured part of being alpha was having very high protective instincts. He'd certainly taken a liking to me quickly enough. "Okay by me."

"Good. We need to do a few things tonight. First, call into work and take tomorrow off." He touched my throat lightly, frowning. "Hector said you'll be well, but there will still be a mark, and it will be hard to explain to your coworkers. And this way you'll have the full weekend to recover."

I grimaced in agreement. "Yeah, okay. You're going to insist I move into this subdivision, aren't you?"

"It's not safe for you at your apartment," he agreed, although not unsympathetically. "For now, stay in my house. I've got a guest bedroom no one's using, and it's better to keep you close until I can figure out what the hell is going on."

I thought about it—about going home and being attacked on the way by vampires stronger than me and not having any allies at hand. Yeah, no. Let's avoid that possible future. "Can I at least pack some stuff up?"

"Sure. I'll go with you. But not tonight, okay? I know you're feeling better, and you certainly look better, but after that kind of blood loss you're likely anemic."

"Change 'likely' for 'definitely' and you'll be closer to the mark," Hector informed us both bluntly. "I want to keep you under observation, Jesse. All right?"

It was really hard to argue with people who had nothing more than your well-being in mind. "Okay, but you think going to work on Monday will be fine?"

"Supernaturals don't usually move much during the day in obvious attacks," Barrett explained patiently. "Too many witnesses. Trouble will start when you leave work in the evening. For the next few weeks, at least, someone will take you to and from work. I'd rather not leave things to chance until we have it in their heads you're part of us now."

So act like a teenager being picked up from school. Got it.

"Tonight, do you feel well enough to go downstairs?" Barrett asked, a touch of worry in his tone. "I want to introduce you to everyone and explain things."

"I really do feel better than I have in a long while," I assured him, meaning every word. It was actually crazy how much better I felt. Blood for the win! "And I'd like to properly say hi."

"All right. Let's do that first. Then I'll deal with Oscar."

Did it make me a bad person to look forward to the shit show that would follow when he did get Oscar on the phone? Maybe I should record it for future listening pleasure.

Marissa and Hector went ahead of us, and Barrett borderline hovered as I climbed out of the bed and headed for the door. I did have some lightheadedness, once I was on my own feet, but I couldn't describe just how indifferent I was to the sensation. I felt *full*, a feeling I'd nearly forgotten. I had a higher energy level, too; it didn't drain me to just stand there and carry my own weight. I felt like a cancer patient who had finally been taken off the treatments and given a new lease on life. I nearly bounced down the stairs, I was so happy.

More people had arrived in the time I'd been recovering, and the living room, dining room, and the patio outside were standing room only. If there were less than two hundred people crammed in here, I would eat my shoes. What were they all doing here? Had they come in to get an explanation of why a vampire attacked another vampire on their territory? We paused on the staircase, not only because it was the only sensible place to stop, but also to give everyone a good look at me, Barrett standing so close our shoulders brushed together.

"Everyone here?" he asked the crowd in general.

"Some of the kids are asleep, but everyone else is here," someone assured him from the bottom of the stairs.

"Good." Barrett took in a breath before pitching his voice to be heard even outside. "I'm sure some of you are wondering what the hell is going on. First, let me introduce the man at my side. This is Jesse. We met him this afternoon. He's clanless, turned by a rogue vampire six years ago—"

There were several hisses and unhappy grumbles, and more than one person shot me a sympathetic look. I found their reaction interesting. Was it something to pity, me out on my own? Is that why they looked at me this way?

"—and we're the first supernaturals he's seen since his turning. I brought him here for safety until we could arrange a meeting with Oscar. Oscar instead sent someone else to meet him, and that person attacked him without provocation. Pretty sure you caught that part," Barrett tacked on dryly, making a few snort in laughter. "Oscar is going to regret his choice tonight because Jesse's a lawyer. He specializes in real estate and tax law."

Someone whistled appreciatively and I could hear a few muted conversations break out. Was it really so odd, having a vampire with marketable skills? Or at least skills that fit in with this modern age?

"Pack." Barrett's tone went firmer, harder, like a commander speaking to his troops. "I have offered Jesse a place in Walker. He has provisionally accepted, as we both agreed it wise to have a trial basis of six months."

People really erupted with questions then. I couldn't pick out all the words, but the tone was incredulous, not irate. They weren't against this? I searched faces, expressions, and they were certainly surprised but not fearful. Not antagonistic. It was just like earlier, when some accepted my presence after just a wave from their alpha. They really weren't at all worried about a vampire staying in their territory?

Barrett held up a hand. "I know you have more than a few questions, and I encourage you to talk to Jesse and ask them. You'll like him too, I think." He cast me a quick wink, and I kid you not, I blushed. Dammit, why were confident men my weakness? "But I want this to be clear. I don't trust the other vampires with him right now, so if he goes out, one of you please go with him. At least for the next several weeks. Also, I need a roster sheet of those willing to be his blood donor. Jesse's been starving for the past six years due to a lack of donors, and I won't let it continue while he's with our pack."

One brave man in the front of the staircase waved a hand to get his alpha's attention. "Barrett, who's he staying with?"

"Me, for now."

Another woman lifted a hand. "You said provisional, but is he just staying here?"

"He's pack until I say otherwise," Barrett answered bluntly.

I looked over the sea of faces and thought about being pack—essentially family—to everyone here. I wasn't sure whether to be overwhelmed or...you know what, overwhelmed about covered it.

Someone finally pitched a question my direction, a pale brunet who bore a striking resemblance to Marissa. "And what do you think about all of this?"

"I think he's crazy, but a good crazy," I answered, the words just popping out of my mouth before I could check them. More than a few snickered and I shrugged, relieved to find Barrett grinning at me. He wasn't the type to be easily offended, apparently. "Look, I said okay to this provisionally because I really don't know much about werewolves, and I didn't think it a good idea to jump into this without knowing anything. But you've been good to me so far, and I'd like to return the favor."

"That's okay by us," a man to my right responded, and good god, did his parents feed him whole cows for breakfast as a child? He was *massive*. He was probably the size of a horse when he shifted. "Where's a signup to be your donor, Jesse?"

"I've no idea," I admitted honestly, and smiled when he gave me an exasperated look. "I'll get something posted to the fridge tonight, how's that?"

"That works."

"Any other questions? No? All right, dismissed." Barrett waved them off and people dispersed.

I regarded them all with some puzzlement. Really? They didn't have any issue with a vampire living in their territory? I could understand if Barrett had a stranglehold on them, but that obviously wasn't the case, as he encouraged questions. Maybe they were just taking a wait-and-see approach. I certainly was.

"Okay, let's get the signup sheet going"—Barrett put his hands on my shoulders, his warm skin like heating pads against my own even through the pullover as he steered me toward the dining room—"and then call Oscar. I'll put you on speaker for the conversation. I'm sure you'll have a few choice words for the man."

"That I do," I agreed darkly.

Marissa, two steps ahead of us, had already stolen a piece of paper from the printer and had scribbled something in marker at the top: *Jesse's donor list. Don't make this kinky, people.* I stopped at the fridge and stared at it, perplexed. "Kinky?"

Clearing his throat, Barrett kept his face and voice admirably neutral as he explained, "There's some interesting stories about blood parties and orgies where vampires are concerned."

"And that's as much as I need to know," I stated decisively. "Thank you, Alpha."

Something that sounded suspiciously like a laugh came from behind us before Luis, one of the two werewolves I'd met downtown, wrote his name on the sheet. He winked at me. "Shame, that. I know a few of the girls were interested in making things fun."

I craned my neck to look at him steadily, not about to back down at his teasing. "I'm afraid I'll be a disappointment to the ladies. Wrong gender for me."

Luis's thick eyebrows shot up. "Vampires can be gay?"

I just looked at him wearily.

Barrett chuckled behind me, a muted sound as if he were trying to hold back but failing. "You stepped right into that one, Luis. There's gay, bi, demi, trans, and asexual werewolves, just like people. Why not vampires?"

"But they're supposed to be famous for seducing virgin girls," Luis protested, and the gleam in his hazel eyes suggested he liked stirring the pot just to get a reaction.

"Their bite is supposed to be an aphrodisiac too, and that's clearly a tall tale," Barrett responded, tone going desert dry. "Thank you for volunteering. Come in the morning."

Shrugging good-naturedly, Luis moved off. I shook my head, wondering aloud, "I'm going to get the question a lot, aren't I?"

Barrett clapped me on the back, subtly moving me toward the dining table again. Was he normally this tactile?

"Probably. To be fair, we don't really know much about vampires, aside from clan politics, territories, and who their leaders are. But when it comes to feeding habits, relationships, and all of that? I probably know as much as you do."

And that wasn't saying much. Well, this should be interesting all around, as they'd expect me to act like a vampire, but really, I was a human who had a vampire body. I wouldn't react as they'd expect.

Marissa supervised a few others signing up. "Jesse, how many times do you feed per day?" she asked over her shoulder.

I stared at her, nonplussed. "Uh, well, technically I eat all day?"

Barrett frowned at my answer, and he and Marissa both stared at me in concern.

That sounded wrong, didn't it? I hastily rectified their assumption. "I have no idea how much blood I'll need per day. I've never had the option before, after all. I normally sip on coconut water throughout the day and then drink, like, a gallon of it for dinner."

"So you don't know," Marissa translated slowly, "if you need three meals a day or if one will suffice."

I nodded in confirmation, hands splayed in a shrug. "No clue."

"Let's err on the side of caution," Hector suggested. I hadn't realized he'd joined in on the conversation, but he stood next to the open doorway of the kitchen, his wide shoulders propped up against the doorframe. "He's in a stage of recovery, after all. He'll likely need more blood than normal. Say, three meals a day. If he's feeling too full, we'll back off and adjust accordingly. I'm pretty sure vampires don't eat three times a day, but it's just rumor. I've no way to confirm it."

Not without asking very pointed questions of another vampire, and no one seemed to think this a good idea. Not even me.

"Three times a day. Okay." Marissa bent back to the feeding chart, organizing people. Was this an occupational habit, the need to see to my diet? I certainly wouldn't argue. She knew these people better than I did.

Barrett pulled out his phone and dialed Oscar's number before putting it on speaker and setting it on the mahogany wood between us. He leaned in, his hand lingering near my forearm. Now that I knew what he tasted like, how it felt to have his hands on me, I was much more aware of him than before. I felt the mildest tingle on my skin and fought it down. Attraction was a rare thing these days. I'd been so hungry, so focused on surviving, I hadn't properly looked at someone in ages. From first sight, I'd considered Barrett handsome, but I initially hadn't really felt much in the way of attraction. He had a very unique look to him with those high cheekbones, and I had a feeling the more you knew about him, the more attractive he became.

The phone rang three times before a clipped British voice answered coolly, "*Walker. You had best have an excellent explanation of why you harmed one of mine.*"

"Oh, I do," Barrett growled, sounding like the wolf he was. "First let's hear your explanation of why your vampire attacked a guest on my territory without warning or provocation."

There was an audible hiccup followed by an irritated reply. "*I beg your pardon? My liaison said he was attacked.*"

"Your liaison hopped out of his SUV, told me he'd 'handle this,' and then attacked Jesse without any warning or provocation." Barrett met my eyes as he said this, inviting me to join if I had something to add.

"Mr. Oscar"—I leaned forward to speak clearly into the phone—"I'm Jesse. I'm afraid that your liaison is twisting the facts in order to cover his ass. Barrett and I were standing in the front yard talking, waiting on him, when he arrived. We didn't even get the man's name or a proper hello out before he attacked me with some sort of bladed weapon. Barrett broke his arm to prevent him attacking again."

"*I see. Jesse, I have two questions for you.*"

From the sound of his voice, it sounded like Blondie was going to be murdered after Oscar hung up the phone. I smiled at the thought. "By all means, please ask."

"*Why did you not properly contact a vampire clan before this?*"

"I didn't even know vampires had clans before today," I answered truthfully. "The rogue vampire who turned me didn't explain anything about vampire society. He covered the general dangers to avoid, how to hunt prey, and then left."

Oscar let out a hissing breath like a cat thrown under a waterfall. "*Might I have the name of the man who turned you?*"

"I only know him by Huxley."

"*The name is not familiar to me. Where were you turned?*"

"Virginia. Just south of Belleview."

A contemplative pause. "*Thank you. I'll, hmm, look further into it and report this matter to the clan in charge of that region. For now, Mr. Jesse, you have my profuse apologies. My liaison swore up and down you were an out-of-control rogue vampire, and he was only fulfilling his duty by quickly exterminating you. That is clearly not the case.*"

Yeah, me still sitting here with the werewolves after the attack and Barrett calling to ream him out was a pretty good indication Blondie screwed up pretty badly. Me calmly answering Oscar's questions put the final nail in the coffin. (Was that a bad pun for a vampire to make?)

"Oscar, I'll be blunt with you. I've offered Jesse a place here in my pack, and he's accepted it." Barrett announced this with smug pleasure. I think he enjoyed saying it a tad too much.

There was a brief splutter from the other vampire. "*Now wait one moment. I agree this matter has been bungled, but a young vampire has no business living with werewolves.*"

*There is much about himself and his new nature he needs to learn. It's entirely unacceptable for him to stay with you."*

Even though Oscar couldn't see it over the phone, Barrett crossed both arms over his chest and glared down at the phone. "I don't trust him with you. For that matter, he doesn't trust vampires at all now. He's only had bad experiences with your people. We're keeping him."

A hint of annoyance started to bleed into Oscar's voice. *"And how do you expect for him to be comfortable with all of you? Your phases during the full moon will be alarming for him to witness. And he can hardly be expected to feed from a werewolf, the very thought is—"* Oscar didn't make a gagging noise, but he came damn close.

Tired of all this posturing, I pulled the phone a little closer and informed him primly, "Actually, werewolves are quite delicious. And this isn't your choice, or Barrett's, but mine. I've made it." I stabbed the phone to end the call. "Posturing prick."

Barrett grinned. "I knew I liked you for a reason. I don't think I've ever heard Oscar so ruffled. He will no doubt try something to winnow his way back into my good graces. To avoid territorial disputes, I'll eventually give in, but we'll worry about it later. For now, let's get you properly settled for the night."

We stood, and I felt like I should say something. "Barrett. Thanks. I know you didn't have to do any of this, and it's going to cause you trouble, so...thanks."

He relaxed into this cocky smile that gave him a slightly bad-boy air. "Welcome to the pack, Jesse."

# 4

As the sunlight filtered in through the bedroom window, I gradually awoke with it, staring at the slate blue wall in front of me with growing confusion. Where was I, again? Walls that color...no, hang on, what state was I in?

Arizona. Right? Right, Flagstaff. I remembered that. But my apartment walls were white, not slate blue, so where—? Oh. Like a flood of information, the scenes of yesterday came pouring through my mind's eye and I took a deep breath. Right. I was now in werewolf territory.

I moved a lot at ten-years-old. My parents had divorced, careers taking them to several different cities, and that meant a lot of houses. I didn't do much better as an adult, at least not until six years ago, when I landed in Flagstaff. You'd think with all my moving experience, I'd be accustomed to waking up in strange places.

Instead, it seemed to just confuse me further.

Seriously, how the hell did I end up here?

Abruptly, I remembered the attack yesterday, and my hand flew to my throat immediately, like it had to verify the wound had closed. It had, seamlessly, which was reassuring. Realizing I'd almost died yesterday was a strange feeling. Like, part of my brain wanted to panic, but I was totally fine? So there was nothing to panic about?

I swear to the god of gay porn, I didn't know how to feel about any of this. Well, except maybe relief in surviving yesterday and being in a safe place. And knowing I'd been accepted by a pack of werewolves after the whole almost-dying thing? Well, that was just icing on the figurative cake.

Flopping onto my back, I took in a deep breath. The sheets smelled freshly laundered, which was nice. The guest bedroom had obviously not been used much, as it had nothing in it aside from a queen-sized bed, a nightstand, and a single landscape on the wall of a twilight forest. The house had at least five bedrooms in it, which seemed a little strange at first glance. I mean, Barrett wasn't married and had no kids, so why so many bedrooms? But I suspected he had them in case something happened—like with me—and people needed to stay under his eye for a while. Part of me liked the fact Barrett wasn't married or with anyone, but that was mostly libido talking. Damn thing was all interested because, to be honest, I really liked the look of Barrett.

I hadn't been with anyone since I being changed—partially because I was afraid of breaking them. Vampire strength was no joke, and it took almost a full year of practice before I stopped accidentally destroying things.

Cars, for instance. Cars were very breakable.

ANYWAY, by the time I'd gotten a handle on my strength, I'd lost a lot of weight and muscle tone because of the not eating thing. At that point, I hadn't even felt attractive, and I was more worried about my health and possibly accidentally killing someone than getting laid, which might be why my libido perked up hopefully now. Barrett was very much my type. He had the warm, charming personality I liked in my boyfriends, plus he was strong enough I wouldn't have to check my strength—I had no reason to hide my vampireness from him. Really, Cupid couldn't have put together a more tempting package if he tried.

But seriously, me, let's not go all damsel for my hero, okay? He probably wasn't even attracted to me. I looked like a walking skeleton right now, after all, and was just a pet project he'd selflessly taken on.

I shook off the brief longing and what-ifs. No, what I needed to focus on right now wasn't Barrett's sexiness but fitting into this pack. And just letting them take care of me didn't sit well. Barrett had made it clear he thought my lawyer skills would come in handy. It was time to figure out how I could be helpful in return.

First, shower.

Barrett had shoved clothes at me last night, so I had something fresh to wear this morning. The jeans and Henley shirt might look odd with my dress shoes, but I wasn't complaining. I hopped into the shower, lathered up, and let the hot water blissfully wash away the bloodstains and stress from the day before. Then I went to pull on the clothes and quickly discovered I had a problem.

Barrett and I were nowhere near the same size. He had five inches of height on me, at least, and was much more muscular. I was emaciated, no other word for it, and the jeans did not want to stay up. I pulled my waistband out a full five inches and frowned. Maybe I should stick with my dress pants this morning.

I moved on to shave, and while staring at myself in the mirror, I noticed some serious changes. For one, the wound across my throat was a healthy pink and closing up faster than I'd have thought possible. Looked like Hector was right, it would be gone completely in no time. I also noticed my overall health bar had definitely improved. My skin no longer looked like a dried-up sponge abandoned in a desert, for one thing, and the sunken look under my eyes had improved by a lot. Wow, who knew just drinking some blood could revive mc so quickly?

I gave up on my hair since I had no product to keep it styled and called it good. Heading downstairs, I found the house strangely empty. Well, maybe not so strange. Everyone was likely having breakfast at their own place and getting ready for work. Only Barrett was at the kitchen bar, on a stool, a half-devoured plate of breakfast in front of him and a cup of coffee in his hand. He looked up and smiled as I came down the stairs. "Hey."

"Morning," I returned, coming to sit next to him.

His brown eyes, slightly golden in the morning light, flicked over me. "Jeans didn't work?"

"Not without a belt," I answered wryly.

"Ah. Should have thought of that." He waved off the concern with a flick of his fingers. "How are you feeling?" His eyes lingered on my throat for a moment, tightening in an unhappy way before his gaze met mine again. Uh oh, was that a look of guilt?

"I'm quite happy with how quickly it's healing." I tried to sound nonchalant, hoping he realized I didn't blame him for what happened, not after he saved and fed me.

"I am too. I'm still mad it happened on my watch, but since you're okay now..." He sighed, and I could see him try and switch mental tracks. "We'll go to your apartment next."

"You're taking me personally?"

"Yeah, figured that was best."

It pleased me to have his focus, and I knew exactly which part of me was pleased about it and mentally smacked it. Down, boy. "And when do you tell me how I can actually pull my weight around here?"

"Today, if you'd like." It was obvious the question made him happy, his mouth curving up in a smile and his eyes tilting up into fine crow's feet. "You know anything about wills?"

"Sure. You can't do tax law without knowing something about inheritance law. They go hand in hand more often than not."

"Good. Then you'll understand when I say we have to change identities every ten to fifteen years, and doing so means we have to set it up so our properties and bank accounts can be inherited"—he put air quotes around the word—"by ourselves?"

It made perfect sense to me. "I've actually started doing that for myself. If you set it up far enough in advance, no one looks at it sideways. The age of the paper trail is what helps make it convincing. Who do I start with?"

"Hector needs help first. He's more complicated because of his doctor's license, and we don't even have a new identity set up for him yet that he can transition into."

That...would take a little research on my part. I didn't know how to transfer a doctor's license or fake it or whatever it was going to take. "Gotcha. I'll have to look up a few things and do some research, but we'll be able to figure it out. Arizona's laws aren't likely to be too different from Virginia's."

His head cocked in curiosity. "You think not?"

"State to state, there's always differences," I admitted easily. "But the bulk of them tend to be the same. Laws are based off precedent and common sense for the most part, and they all came from the same original law book, too. It means there's not a ton of variation. Some, and I always double-check something if I'm in a different state, but I'm not usually too surprised."

"Good. That was one of the things I worried about when we pulled up stakes to move here." Barrett went back to his eggs, forking them into his mouth.

The back door abruptly opened without warning and Luis strolled in. "I'm here."

So he was my first donor, eh? I stood almost automatically. "Thanks for this, Luis."

"No prob," he assured me, closing the door behind him. "Where do you want me?"

Good question.

"Sit at the bar," Barrett directed, scraping up the last bite from his plate.

Both of us sitting seemed a good idea, and the bar would even out our height to not make the angle awkward. I grabbed some napkins from a decorative wooden box nearby just in case, then sat. Luis wore short sleeves—nothing to impede me—and he handed me his wrist without any fanfare. I took it, then stared at the skin with something akin to panic. Last night, they'd used a scalpel to open their skin for me, but

I'd been too weak to make any other option viable. But did I just...I mean, biting in seemed like it would hurt.

A warm hand pressed between my shoulder blades and Barrett's voice rumbled low in my ear as he said, "Breathe. Jesse, breathe."

I sucked in a breath and felt foolish almost instantly. "Sorry. I just realized I have no idea how to do this."

"You really haven't fed from anyone before last night." Luis said it as a statement more than a question. I looked up to find him watching me steadily, his hazel eyes not judging, but thoughtful. "Dude, your willpower must be something else."

"I didn't want to hurt anyone." My eyes closed as I sought my equilibrium. I couldn't begin to describe how I loathed the thought of hurting someone, even by accident, but especially in cases like this, when the person was trying to help me.

"You're worried about biting in?" Barrett asked gently.

Nodding, I gestured helplessly to his wrist. "I could do muscle damage if I go too deep."

"Even if you use a knife to open a vein, it'll still smart," Luis said in a very practical tone. "It's okay, man. Werewolves heal fast, and I'm tougher than most if you do go too deep. Think of me as your guinea pig, okay?"

I might owe this man dinner later. Scratch that, I knew I did. I gathered up my courage from somewhere and lifted his wrist to my mouth. It smelled good, like a delectable dessert or a roast slowly cooking. Instinct made me lick the skin, and it tasted good too, but frustrating, as it blocked me from what I really wanted. Carefully, I sank my canines into his flesh, a little alarmed by how easily the skin gave under the pressure. Then sweet warmth flooded my mouth, and I stopped worrying about it for a moment.

"Huh. You're right, Barrett," Luis observed to his alpha, "this kinda feels good. Maybe the orgy party stories aren't too far off."

"You would say that." Barrett sounded half amused, half exasperated. "I assume there's some kind of vampire chemistry going on to make it pleasant for us."

Good to hear. I'd forgotten to tell him to let me know if he felt lightheaded—I would stop if so—but surely he had the common sense to tell me.

It felt incredibly nice to eat and fill my stomach without that vaguely dissatisfied gnawing sensation. Still, I was cautious about eating too much at once. I didn't want to cause trouble for Luis. When I felt mostly satisfied, I stopped and pulled back, licking any trace of blood from his skin before withdrawing entirely. Then I grabbed the napkins, cleaning him up better.

"That couldn't have been enough." Luis had the same squinty-eyed look on his face Barrett had worn last night. Hell, Barrett sported it now.

"I'm actually full," I assured them both, meaning it. "I think my appetite shrunk over the years. It'll take a while to build it back up."

"Four ounces of blood and he's full," Barrett grumbled to no one in particular. "Damn, I'm glad we stumbled across you when we did. All right, Luis, you handle things at the site today. Call me if there's a problem, and I can swing by."

"Sure thing." Luis hopped off the stool and gave me a firm look. "And you, don't faint."

"Excuse you," I retorted without heat, "I have never fainted in my life. Except yesterday, when I was stabbed, and being stabbed is a perfectly valid excuse to lose it for a few minutes."

Barrett shook his head as he exchanged a look with Luis that communicated volumes, although I couldn't unpack it all.

"Good call," Luis told him.

"Yup. See you tonight." Barrett waved him out, already in motion to wash up breakfast dishes.

Okay, seriously, what had I just missed? The door opened and closed as Luis left, leaving just the two of us in the kitchen. "I take it you two don't agree about the stabbing-fainting thing."

"You never should have been so easy to take down," Barrett explained as he soaped up a sponge, his eyes on his hands. "Hector had some really choice words after you went to bed last night about how malnourished you are."

I rubbed the back of my neck and wondered how to respond.

"But what Luis really meant," Barrett continued, washing out his coffee mug, "was that you're too gentle by nature. I'm not actually sure you'd survive well in a vampire clan. You don't have the ruthless nature to climb on top of people."

"There's a reason why I went into the part of law that doesn't require court appearances," I agreed with a shrug. I wasn't actually good at arguing with people. I lost steam before I could get a full argument out. Could I stand my ground if I needed to? Of course, I wasn't a doormat, but I tended to avoid conflict if I could find a more peaceful way out. "Is that really what vampire clans are like, though? Dog eat dog?"

"Every vampire I've ever met was cutthroat, let me put it that way. Oscar is by far the most laid back of them, and even he's callous." Rinsing the plate, he put it on the rack to dry before toweling his hands.

I studied him carefully. I instinctively sensed something about this man, even if I couldn't put my finger it. "Barrett, answer me honestly. Did I trigger your protective instincts?"

He stopped dead, head coming up sharply in surprise. "How did you know?"

"Alpha of a pack of wolves, of course your protective instincts run high." Bracing my forearms against the bar, I leaned against it, meeting his eyes and feeling my mouth curl up in amusement. "Anyone you think of as 'yours' will automatically fall under that need to protect. I realized last night I must have done so—you'd never have extended the offer to join your pack otherwise—although I'm not quite sure why you took a liking to me so quickly. Unless, of course, this is another instinctual thing where you looked at me as a potential threat that you can neutralize by turning me into an ally instead."

He stared at me hard, expression not giving anything away, for several taut seconds. Then he blew out a breath. "Yeah, you're a lawyer, all right."

I grinned at him cheekily. "Legal training makes you think from both perspectives. I'm right, aren't I?"

"Dead on," he agreed, shaking his head, more amused than offended. "Did you agree because you realized all of that?"

"Partially. And also because I was afraid of what would happen to me if I stayed out there on my own without allies." Perhaps I should have said more about my past earlier. In my defense, a lot had happened last night, and I'd been reeling and trying to keep up with it all. Still, this man had opened his home up to me, and that was owed some consideration. "I...think I should tell you something. I'm sure you wondered how a rogue turned me. Why he stayed and taught me anything afterward."

Barrett came around the bar to stand next to me, close enough his body heat radiated and warmed me in return. I wondered what it was about werewolves having no concept whatsoever of personal space. His concern was an open thing across his face, drawing his brows and mouth together into taut lines. "I have wondered, but you don't have to relive bad memories."

Shaking my head, I whispered past a constricting throat, "This might tie in to today. I don't know for sure, but you deserve to be forewarned. And forearmed. A group of black witches had captured Huxley for some sort of ritual, but he grew too weak to survive the full rite, so they captured me to feed him, to keep him alive. I'd had a flat tire and no spare and was walking to a gas station for help when they nabbed me off a dark country road. It was a shock to me, to learn that the supernatural world was all too real—and then realizing I was to be the vampire's snack? It was...not a feeling I like to remember. Anyways, neither of us liked the idea of me being Huxley's snack and then a corpse, and to make a very long story short, he decided to turn me instead, so I could break us both out. It worked, we escaped, and he stayed with me for two days to gather his strength. During bouts of consciousness, he taught me the basics. I woke up one morning to find him gone."

Those expressive eyes of Barrett's closed as he hissed out a few choice words. For the black witches or for the rogue vampire, I wasn't sure which. I cursed them both frequently.

I sketched on a smile, but it felt so unnatural I let it drop again. "Six years ago, I didn't know enough to question matters and could barely focus beyond learning to survive. But if there's more witches in this area? If there's the possibility of dark practitioners here, then you should know. They don't always play by the rules."

Without warning, Barrett hauled me into a hug. He meant to be supportive, but on some level, I suspected he wanted to keep me close. I sort of just melted because dammit, I needed a hug. For six years, I'd never told another soul what happened to me, had never truly grieved for myself. Barrett's warm embrace was solid and grounding and precisely what my heart needed.

"Damn, Jesse. Just damn. Thank you for telling me. You're right, I can take better precautions knowing this. I don't know much about the witches who recently moved in, but apparently I need to rectify this pronto."

It felt liberating to have my story out. I felt more relaxed now that he knew, although I didn't fully understand why. "I'll help in any way I can."

"I think you can access more information than me at the moment. You have access to the court system's records, right?"

I nodded in confirmation he didn't need. "Sure. When we get my laptop, I'll dive in and do some research."

"Let's head to your apartment, then. I'd prefer to be in and out quickly, so just get what you need for the next two weeks or so. We'll take you moving in with us in stages."

That went without saying. I mean, where would they even put me long term? Every house in the subdivision had its own family, or so I'd been led to understand, except the three still needing repairs. I could certainly stay in Barrett's guest bedroom for a while, but clearing out my apartment would mean I needed more space than just one room. I'd been through so many transitional phases in my life, I decided not to question this one too much. It would work out, things always did.

# 5

It didn't even take an hour to go to my apartment, pack the essentials, and come back. I set up shop at the dining room table, working steadily on my laptop and snagging Barrett's home printer before digging into my research. I quickly realized the doctor's license would definitely be the hardest part of creating a new identity for Hector, as there was no legal way to transfer it. Understandably. The only feasible way was if he changed his name, and it might work because few people really dug deep into an identity. If you met a doctor in his office and saw his medical license on the wall, you took it as truth. So long as the government systems didn't throw up an error while he did taxes and applied for medical license renewals, we'd be hunky dory.

Hmm, how to do this quasi-legal? That would be the best method, as we'd raise less red flags that way.

A tap on my shoulder brought my head around, and I blinked up at Barrett. "Problem?"

"It's past lunchtime," he answered, somewhat exasperated. "Do you not have an appetite?"

"Pretty sure it's broken at this point," I admitted lightly. Glancing at the clock above the sink, I realized it was past one p.m. No wonder he'd prodded me. "All right, who's for lunch?"

Sitting down in the chair next to me, he extended his arm. "Me."

"Uh, no," I denied quickly. "I fed on you last night. It cannot be healthy to do so again already."

"Werewolf, remember?" Barrett looked at me steadily, patiently. He must have a wealth of patience to handle two hundred people on a regular basis. "I heal very quickly."

I stared at the bared bronze skin in front of me with a strange mix of hunger and doubt. "Are you really sure?"

"Jesse, will you just eat already?" Barrett sounded exactly like an exasperated mother with a picky three-year-old.

Rolling my eyes, I muttered, "Yes, Mom."

He chuckled in response. "I feel like it some days."

"I bet." Feeding still felt new and unnerving to me, and I sucked in a breath for courage before lifting his wrist to my mouth and carefully biting in, then immediately wanted to groan. He was really, truly delicious, even more so than the first time. I wasn't sure how, exactly. His blood had more...body to it? A deeper sense of flavor? I sounded like a wine connoisseur, but I didn't know how else to describe it. If he were chocolate, he'd be the dark kind, the one that was mostly cocoa and creamy. I also felt more comfortable feeding from him than I had with Luis and the others. There wasn't any reason for it, but the feeling persisted.

I licked the wound clean, not wanting to waste a drop, and started to pull back.

"Oh no you don't, mister," Barrett scolded. "That was less than what you had for breakfast. Go another minute at least."

Seriously, he sounded just like a mother. Amused, I resisted the urge to say something smart alecky. I'd stopped because I really did feel satisfied, but he was right in that this was less than I'd had from Luis. If I wanted to regain my weight and strength, I needed to eat more. At least a little.

He finally allowed me to draw back, and I honestly felt myself slide into that gluttonous state where a nap sounded good. Apparently, feeding on werewolf was not unlike eating a Thanksgiving turkey. "Thank you."

"You're welcome." Dropping his wrist to his lap, carefully right-side up to avoid smearing blood on his pants while his skin healed, he jerked his chin to indicate my piles and piles of paper. "How goes it?"

"Mm, well, some of this I already knew." I had to fight the food coma as I pointed to my stacks of paper. "We can register birth certificates with the registrar of the county, and Hector can sign those as 'attending physician' and get the ball rolling on new identities. Once we have a birth certificate in place, we can get social security numbers easily, and from there things are more or less a snap. I'll periodically update the records so we have immunizations, school history, and so on. Hector will have to help sign anything medical. We'll create bank accounts as well. I'm still researching how to deal with Hector's medical license. Has he needed to transfer it before?"

Barrett dashed my hopes by shaking his head. "No, Hector's only seventy years old. His license is due to expire in the next five years, hence our concern, but he's got no experience transferring it to a new identity."

"Hmm. Rats, I'd hoped he'd done this before and could give me an idea. I think the easiest thing to do is to put in for a name change and then fudge the dates. I'm not sure, though, it'll take some more research and thought on my part. But today"—I gestured broadly toward the paperwork—"I'd like to get about twenty identities started. The sooner we do that, the easier it is down the road. Who needs one next?"

"We're actually all in decent shape except Hector." Barrett sat and thought about it for a moment. "Most of us took advantage of the move to change names and such, as no one would know us here. I guess I'll send you the twenty oldest members who need some prep for the next round?"

"Yeah, that's probably the best way to start. I need to know what names, birthdays, and so on they want on the paperwork. They'll be the ones who have to remember it all."

"True. Okay, I'll make some phone calls and help you get started." Barrett dug out his phone and then paused, giving me the sharp evaluating stare he sometimes did. "What about your license?"

"Haven't figured it out either," I admitted sourly. "I'd rather not take the bar exam again, but it might come down to it. We'll see. I have plenty of time to think about it, as I only recently moved here and people know I should be thirty-three."

"You're not, though?" His tone lilted up in question.

"Technically," I answered with a shrug.

He gave a hum, then picked up his phone and made those calls.

We spent the rest of the day working together to build a future for his pack. I liked it. I hadn't been able to openly be me, in all my weirdness, for years. So much of what I could do, see, sense, even feel had to be capped at human levels. I'd always hid part of myself while in public. Here, I could catch a sheet of paper before it fluttered off the table with inhuman reflexes and Barrett didn't find it odd. Here, I could react to the conversation he had on the phone, even when he didn't put it on speaker, and he didn't question why I could hear it all so clearly.

It was incredibly relaxing.

I knew the instant the school bus must have let the kids out at the neighborhood, as the front door abruptly crashed open before several small bodies tumbled through. Barrett didn't even look, just continued as he had been, ignoring the furry bodies that raced through the kitchen and out the back door, heading for the pool.

Watching them go, I finally asked the question that had bothered me. "So...I take it you don't need a full moon to change over."

"Nope. The call to transform is much stronger on those nights, hence the legend. The younger members have a hard time staying human, but we change back and forth at will." Barrett shrugged casually, although his eyes watched me sharply under his dark eyebrows. "Surely you have more questions than that."

"Well, yeah," I admitted, rubbing the back of my neck and wondering how frank I could be. "But some of it is selfish curiosity, and some of it I'm pretty sure is rude to ask, and I'm still trying to figure out how I fit in with all of you. I'll figure stuff out as I go along."

He propped his chin in his hand, leaning against the tabletop as he studied me. Barrett's dark brown eyes were incredibly penetrating when he really focused on something, like now. I had the vague sense I should squirm or duck away from him, but something kept me from doing so, and I stared levelly back. I could see in the slight curve of his mouth how this pleased him. "For all that you're polite and nonconfrontational, you do have a spine of steel. Not many can look an alpha werewolf in the eye. That's good. If you do choose to go into a vampire clan at some point, odds are you won't become a doormat."

"But you don't think I'll thrive there, either," I observed, canting my head in question.

"No." His eyes remained on me, evaluating. "Like I said before, you're not ruthless enough. You need a lot of ambition and bloodthirsty resolve to make it in a vampire clan. Or so I've seen. It's why I offered you a place with us, which I grant you is strange, the races don't mix like this normally, but..." He shrugged, adequately displaying he didn't care what the world thought of his decision.

"I don't mind if it's strange," I assured him softly. Feeling a little shy, I admitted more slowly, "And I like it. Having a safe place."

"You need to stop saying things like that." He groaned, dropping his head so he held his forehead. "Look, Jesse. Werewolves are very, very tactile. If you haven't figured it out yet, we have no concept of personal space. And when you say things like that, it makes us just want to hug you for a few hours."

"Hmmm." I pretended to consider this. "Be hugged by nice-looking people. Wow, not sure if I can survive it."

He might have snorted a laugh before throwing an arm around my shoulders and snagging me, hauling me into his chest for a hug. It was an awkward angle, with us both in the chairs, but I went with it. Earlier was the first time I'd been hugged in, well, years. And now I was getting another? Go, me! I'd been starving for touch as much as food, to be honest, and Barrett smelled fantastic. I said that as a man, not just a vampire.

I leaned into him with a sigh of pleasure, my arms coming up to gently hold his waist. Yeah, I could definitely get used to this.

"Oooh, please tell me I'm interrupting something," a new voice chimed in, sounding lecherous and amused.

Pulling back, I blinked up at the young woman. She looked vaguely like Barrett, with the same thick black hair, dark brown eyes, and high cheekbones, but more youthful and with a dusting of freckles over her nose.

"Ria," Barrett greeted in a martini-dry tone. "Jesse, this is my younger sister, Ria. She thinks it's funny to dig at me, so ignore her usually inappropriate comments."

"I happen to have a thing for forbidden love, and a male werewolf and vampire pairing would be the epitome of that," Ria explained brightly, her whipcord thin body bouncing in place with false exuberance. "So tell me I was interrupting something?"

"Nice to meet you, Ria," I responded smoothly. "And I doubt half-starved vampire is your brother's type."

"Actually," she answered with impish delight, "his type is— Oww! What the hell, Barrett, don't step on my foot like that! I'm attached to it."

"You won't be for much longer unless you stop," he growled at her. And I do mean growled. I swear his vocal cords changed so he could put the right growl into it. "Now. I texted you for a reason. Jesse will need to partner up with you to set up the new identities for the pack."

"Sweet, so you're working on that?" Ria—whom I now looked at properly—had a geeky vibe to her. It might be the yellow-tinted, thick-framed black glasses on her nose giving her that appearance, or maybe the oversized sweatshirt and casual flip-flops, as if she only dressed for comfort and nothing else.

To me, Barrett explained, "Ria is our computer guru. She keeps track of everyone's movements, tries to stay on top of the other territories, and does whatever hacking needs to be done. She tackled most of the identity changes during this last move, and I heard much grumbling because of it."

"I'm a hacker, not a lawyer," Ria complained to him in a tone suggesting she'd said it at least several hundred times.

Looking toward the heavens in a clear bid for patience, Barrett replied wearily, "Yes, Ria. I heard you the first thousand times. But you managed all right, didn't you?"

"Yeah, barely. I'd much rather Jesse do it."

"For that matter"—I gave her a grin—"Jesse would much rather Jesse do it, too. But I'd like your help in setting up the new bank accounts. I don't know what bank you'd prefer to use, after all."

"We tend to do everything online these days." Ria put a finger to her full lips and looked me over. "Shouldn't we feed you first?"

I blinked at her, then glanced at the clock on the wall. It wasn't even four yet. "Isn't it a little early for dinner?"

"He had a late lunch," Barrett explained to her. "Maybe later."

Not bothered, she shrugged. "Let me know when you're hungry. You want to come to my lair tomorrow? A little late to start in on things today, and we'll have all weekend."

"Sure, that's fine. Uh, where's your lair?"

Ria pointed a finger dead ahead of her. "Right next door. Just come over when you're ready."

"Sure." I might have added something else, but a ripple of snarls came from the front door like a tidal wave of warnings. Barrett shot out of his chair, already halfway to the door before I could untangle myself from the laptop cord and follow him.

I didn't see anything threatening at first—not counting the thirty werewolves either changed over into furry form or snarling out the open front door—but eventually I got the right angle to see the dark SUV parked out front. It didn't take a genius to figure out someone had come calling unannounced. The question was: weres, vampires, or witches?

Luis came in to stand right behind me, and I didn't think it was my imagination that he'd moved into the position to serve as my guard. "I'm already so used to smelling Jesse, I tuned them out until they got close," he said to the room in general, sounding vaguely put out.

"You're not the only one," Barrett reassured him. Well, he likely meant it to be reassuring, but he had a hard look in his eyes and a flat tone to his voice. His attention never wavered from the SUV. "Jesse, I'd prefer it if you stayed in the house until I see who this is and what they want."

Seeing the sense in that, I nodded. "Okay."

With a grateful look at me, he swiftly exited the house, standing within six feet of the vehicle. He planted his feet and said in a low tone, "You dare much to just waltz onto our territory."

The door slowly opened and a short man with unruly dark hair stepped out, carefully keeping his body language calm, but he had an air of agitation. He looked otherworldly to me, like Huxley had, his skin a paler porcelain than human skin could attain, his movements smoother, much like a dancer's. I'd never been able to view myself from the outside before, but it made me wonder, did I move like that? Look that way? "I didn't think you'd answer if I called," he said in a distinctly British accent.

Oh. This must be Oscar. I recognized the voice.

"I might not have, but it would have still been a better decision than what you're doing now." Barrett heaved out a gusty sigh, sounding beyond irritated, and the entire pack went doubly alert. I had to think it was a mannerism he did before shit really hit the fan. "All right, Oscar. You're here. I'll give you two minutes to say your piece, then you leave."

Oscar seemed amused at this, if the eloquent lift of a brow was anything to go by. "You think we can discuss this in two minutes. Very well, let's attempt it. I wish to speak with our young vampire."

"You mean you want to speak to my vampire, and you're flat out of luck," Barrett retorted. Part of me warmed at hearing the words "my vampire" out of his mouth. "Anything else?"

"Alpha, do see reason. He's young. You informed me of his unfortunate turning by a rogue. There's much he needs to know, to learn, and only another vampire can adequately see to his education. It's even worse he's arrived in such a poor state." Oscar's eyes shifted unerringly straight at me, and even with the awkward angle of a wall and doorway blocking most of his view, he studied what he could of me, and his expression became patronizing. "A very poor state."

Have you ever met someone and wanted to buy them a taser for their bathtub? It wasn't what they said, per se, but how they said it? The condescending, slightly arrogant way they looked at someone that just irritated the fuck out of you. I felt the distinct urge to wrap both hands around his throat and restrict the airway. I didn't think I was alone in this, as quite a few grumbles came from the people around me.

I had about as much desire to follow this man as I did to stalk a serial killer.

Oscar didn't seem to realize my feelings toward him. He kept talking to Barrett as if he was the only one who needed to be convinced. "Mr. Jesse needs to be taught how to properly feed. How to manage his new body, how to make the right connections in the vampire world in order to make his way through it. Staying, hmm, here..."—the way he said "here" was filled with distaste, and wow, it seemed the mask was off—"will not help him achieve any of this. It's understandable that you took him in, werewolves are such pack animals. I quite see how your instincts came into play in this case, but it's really not suitable, Alpha Barrett."

Barrett didn't respond. With his back to me, I couldn't read what he was thinking from his expression, but his body language shouted tension. I didn't want him to think Oscar was right. Well, Oscar actually did have a few good points, but it wasn't like I was interested in going with the man. I'd rather shoot myself.

I moved three steps exactly, to stand outside of the door, still obeying Barrett's wishes to stay out of reach of the other vampires but in full view to give my own opinion on all of this. "Barrett."

He turned his head, and I could read the conflict on his face. I made my resolve audible. "I have no wish to go with him."

Barrett softened a touch, just enough to give me a faint, approving smile. "All right. Oscar, your two minutes are up."

Oscar bristled openly, staring at me like I'd lost my mind. "I realize you are young and ignorant, but you cannot possibly think staying here will be beneficial to you! You need to learn how to live properly as a Vampire."

I could hear the capital "V." "Mr. Oscar, you misstepped, vitally so, when you sent a minion out to meet me. In that one instance, I learned what it will really be like for me inside a vampire clan. I don't want to live the rest of my life in conflict. The Walker Pack is a family. A warm, generous, happy family. I have no enemies here. I will stay with them for as long as they will have me."

Jaw dropping, Oscar stared at me for a long moment. I didn't think he expected this kind of resistance. Perhaps he thought Barrett held me like some sort of hostage, or bartering chip. Maybe he held the opinion I was there as a pawn in a power struggle and thought he could advance by showing up in person and throwing some words around. He never expected I would choose to stay, or that the werewolves around me would encourage it.

"Go, Oscar." The alpha spoke in a tone encouraging direct and instant obedience.

Oscar glared at him, the sharpness in the expression nearly lethal. "When you've come to your senses, call me and we will discuss this again."

Crossing his arms over his chest, Barrett stared him down. "I'll pencil that in. How does never sound?"

Ignoring him, Oscar appealed directly to me. "You will see soon this is a mistake. Call me and I will arrange to pick you up myself. I will arrange for you a good mentor. You won't lack for guidance."

He made it sound like I needed a master for my grasshopper self. And maybe, to him, I did. But you didn't use this tone when addressing another adult. Really, I did not like this man.

Seeing the futility of staying there any longer, he blew out a breath and climbed back into the SUV. A moment later, it reversed out of the driveway and retreated back the way it had come in.

Barrett came to stand directly in front of me. He seemed perturbed but also happy, as if I had surprised him in the best of ways. "You really have no intention of leaving?"

"With that douche?" I snorted and shook my head. "No way. Although if this causes you trouble, and I do need to leave, just say the word. I'll move somewhere else."

Luis barked out a laugh. "Even if it does mean trouble for you to stay, you'll stay anyway. You're pack now, Jesse. You said as much, and we don't abandon our own."

Well. I grinned up at him, pleased. I think I was just officially adopted.

# 6

I went to Ria's "lair" the next morning with my laptop tucked under my arm and two file folders, ready to work. Her house was much like her brother's in style, the same stucco building on the outside with beige carpets and cherry wood cabinets in the living room entertainment center. I noticed she'd painted the walls something other than blue, though; hers had different shades of muted greens and brown. She had a nice eye for color, as it looked good.

Werewolves, I had discovered, had an open-door policy. They never locked their doors and they didn't expect people to knock. You just walked in and announced yourself if you were going to stay for longer than two minutes. It did not feel natural for me to do so, but I gamely did anyway as I cleared the door. "Ria, I'm here!"

"Oh good, come up!" she encouraged from somewhere above me.

I followed the carpeted stairway to the second level and found the loft area upstairs had been converted to something that looked a lot like a bat cave. Monitors were all along one wall, and two desks held multiple keyboards and towers. In the midst of this spiderweb of technology sat Ria, her sweats-covered legs crossed in an executive office chair, breakfast burrito in one hand and a coffee cup in the other. She waved me to a chair next to her with the burrito, swallowing before asking, "You eat yet?"

"I did," I assured her, taking the chair. Then I had to adjust the lever up to accommodate my longer legs since Ria ran on the short side.

She made a show of looking me up and down, clearly doubtful.

"I'll have you know I had to wear my loosest pair of jeans today because everything else is uncomfortably tight," I informed her. I was both proud and relieved about this. "According to the scale, I've gained five pounds in the three days I've been here."

Concern eased from her face. "That's great. Marissa knows this, right?"

"Marissa weighed me," I answered, grinning. "I think I've become her favorite project."

"Food is serious business to her, so it doesn't surprise me." Taking a sip of her coffee, she kept studying me.

I knew that look. "Ria, just spit it out."

She didn't, pondering another moment before coming to some internal resolution. With a nod, she finally opened her mouth. "I don't know if you realized it, but you made us all really happy yesterday. I mean *really* happy. Vampires have always had this holier-than-thou attitude in the supernatural world. Because they live longer than we do, and they're stronger, they tend to be pricks."

I carefully watched her as she spoke, and her expression, her body language, said more than her words expressed. She was happy, yes, but questioning. She didn't understand why I'd stayed with them. How engrained was this prejudice? "I caught part of that. Oscar's arrival yesterday spoke volumes. He's not even the master of a vampire clan, but he waltzed into Walker territory without invitation and tried making demands like it was natural to expect Barrett to obey him. I figured some of it was just posturing, but not all of it could be explained by that."

"So you do understand what it meant when you chose us instead?"

"That I feel werewolves, this pack specifically, is better than the local vampire clan. Yeah, I know. But Ria, the Walker Pack helped and welcomed me when no one else would. I think it's natural I choose you over them."

She nodded, not disagreeing, but not agreeing either. "But still, that's not how everyone else saw it. The only thing they realized was you thought Oscar a prick—good call, he just showed everyone how much he is—and you chose Barrett as your leader over a vampire. It made us happy, yeah, because it's not every day a vampire thinks a werewolf is better than his own kind. But Barrett was worse than a peacock, he strutted around so much. He was so smug it was unbearable. I nearly hit him just to deflate his ego."

I grinned, as I'd caught him preening more than once. Of course, I hadn't attributed his attitude to me, per se, I'd just assumed he was smug about giving Oscar the finger. Since she was being so frank with me, I decided to ask questions I hadn't quite found the timing for with Barrett. "Ria, I've got two burning questions."

"Shoot," she encouraged.

"First, I'm really not a burden to all of you, am I?"

"What, with the feeding? No, not really. Taking ten minutes out of our day to feed you is no biggie, and you're seriously saving our bacon with all of the legal help. We consider it a total win-win. Even if Oscar decides to throw a tantrum about you being here, he can't force the issue on his own. He doesn't have the means to overrule Barrett, especially with you freely choosing to stay here."

"That segues nicely into my next question. Can someone force me out of here?"

Ria pursed her lips thoughtfully. "Hmm. Yes and no. Technically, yes. If a master vampire from one of the clans came in and demanded we give you over, it would come down to a fight, and we're honestly not big enough to win that kind of fight. Vampires fight dirty. We'd fight for you, of course, but I'm not sure we'd win. But short of an actual battle, no. There's no way to force you out of here, and honestly? Most vampire clans won't be so determined to have you that they'd risk exposure by fighting. You're just one vampire. A skilled, educated vampire, sure, and that's a good commodity. But still."

"Just one vampire," I repeated. It was what I had hoped to hear, and I trusted she'd made this statement based on her own experience in this world and the information she constantly gathered for her brother and the pack.

"That ease your worries some?" Ria smiled in understanding.

"Yes, thank you."

"Good. Then, one more piece of information for you. My brother's bisexual and you're exactly his type."

If I'd been drinking something, I would have choked. As it was, my eyes bugged out of my head and my jaw flapped around as I croaked. "You're jerking my chain."

Grinning in wolfish amusement, she shook her head in a deliberate side to side motion. "Nooope. He's bisexual, leans toward guys. And he loves—adores—the intellectuals. A soft spoken, gentle-natured intellectual is literally in his target zone."

I was half convinced she was still jerking my chain, but only half. "Is that why you were teasing him yesterday?"

"Exactly why," she purred, wagging her eyebrows suggestively. "Feel free to prove me right."

"How about when I look less like a breathing skeleton, I'll think about it?" I grinned when she gave an exasperated sigh. "Hard to have game when the man acts like a mother hen and tries to feed me every time I'm in his orbit. That does not lead to sexy times."

Making a face, she grumbled, "Okay, point. He really does that with you?"

"Yup," I answered, popping the "P."

"Well damn. I mean, in his defense, it's a love language for our family, but all right, fine. Get your health back up, then prove me right."

I didn't think it was likely to happen, which was something of a shame, as Barrett was very attractive. I wouldn't mind if something clicked between us, but Barrett struck me as someone who put the pack first, which meant he likely needed a female alpha. And I was definitely not that. Could never be that.

Feeling like we needed a change of topic, I gestured to a free space of desk near her. "Can I set up there?"

"Sure. What are we doing this morning?"

"Well, I talked to people last night, and I got birthdays and names and stuff. Hector signed all the birth certificates I prepared and promised to drop them off at the registrar's office himself. So today, I guess check the system to see if we're good to go on getting social security numbers, and maybe start bank accounts if we can. If not, help me figure out how to transfer both a doctor's license and my attorney's license. I'm not sure how to do that."

"Likely will take a little hacking." Crumpling up her burrito wrapper, she tossed it with unerring accuracy for the garbage can on the other side of the room, making a clean shot. "Sounds fun. Let's get rolling."

After six hours of staring at a computer screen, my eyes felt dry and itchy. We decided to call it quits after figuring out the main problem. There was no help for it, Ria would have to hack into the different databases and then manually enter in new license information for both me and Hector. It was the answer I'd expected, really, and it was just as well that Ria wanted to try a few tricks before throwing in the towel.

Ria and I agreed the rest could wait until Monday. I loaded up the folders and my laptop in hand and wandered out of her house and back toward Barrett's. I idly thought of eating something, since I'd skipped lunch. A fact no one would be pleased about, but I honestly hadn't noticed the lunch hour whizzing by until we chose to stop and realized the time. Oops.

Four steps out the door, my ears caught a heated argument going on. Two of the pack members stood in a driveaway on the opposite side of the cul-de-sac yelling at each other, gesturing angrily toward the back end of a truck that looked as if it had been hit by something. A pity, as it was clearly a new truck. No one else was outside, and the argument grew more and more heated as I watched.

I knew for a fact Barrett did not like this sort of behavior, as he'd mentioned hating infighting. He was out on a job, but if he'd been here and seen this, he would have stopped it. I didn't think it my place to go over there and break up the fight, but I didn't want to see them go at each other's throats, either. Wavering, I hesitated a moment too long, and the shorter of the two shoved the other hard.

Okay, no. Someone had to intervene.

Putting everything down on a nearby boulder, I darted across the street, calling loudly as I moved. "No! Stop, stop, stop."

Both of them paused, turning toward me with livid expressions. I didn't know the name of either, but this didn't stop me. Actually, it might be a good way to help insert myself into the argument.

The taller, burlier man took a step toward me. "This doesn't concern—"

Holding his eye, I held out a hand while cutting in. "I haven't met you yet. I'm Jesse, and you are?"

He growled, irritated I'd cut him off, but reluctantly took my hand. His skin was hot and calloused compared to mine. "Matias."

"Pleasure, Matias," I replied, and even meant it. Withdrawing, I offered a handshake to the other. "And you?"

"Oron," he answered, and I didn't mistake his relief.

"Pleasure, Oron." I smiled at them in turn, ignoring the hostile tension reeking from both of them. "Now, what's the argument about?"

"This doesn't require your interference," Matias bit out, trying to loom over me.

His alpha did a better job at looming despite being a hair shorter. I was not impressed. I locked eyes with him, and he flinched first. "I'm arbitrating this argument before you two get into a physical altercation. Consider it a favor because if we can settle this before Barrett's back, he won't know that you were *this* close"—I held up my finger and thumb a scant distance apart—"to fighting each other. We both know he won't be pleased about it. Fighting a pack member is never a good decision. Now, what's the argument about?"

They both stared at me hard as if wanting to argue but not wanting me to go away. I think Oron, at least, didn't want this to escalate, but he looked flushed and embarrassed. Too ashamed to answer me?

Reluctantly, he pried his mouth open and admitted, "I borrowed my brother's truck and, um, backed into something."

"You borrowed my truck *without permission*," Matias corrected sharply, glaring with lethal intensity, "after I specifically told you not to drive it, when you have your own truck to drive, and then you backed into a telephone poll with it."

All right, I could understand the ire now. "Oron. Why did you drive his truck?"

"Had a flat tire on mine, and my spare's flat too." Oron hunched farther into himself, like a turtle without a shell. He looked perhaps eighteen to me, but the action made him appear incredibly young in that moment, just a kid called out by the adults. "I, uh, was taking the tire to get it fixed."

"And this wasn't something that could wait until Matias had returned? Because I'm sure that if you'd explained the situation, he would have helped fix the tire." Or at least I hoped so.

Hunching even further in on himself, Oron admitted in a small voice, "I have a date tonight. I didn't want to be late."

The plot thickened. "You understand that because you were so hasty and careless, you now get to pay for fixing Matias's bumper, correct?"

"I also have a date tonight," Matias grumped, his ire simmering down slightly. "I'm taking her to a nice place, and I don't want to show up in a banged-up truck."

Plot twist times two. I rubbed my jaw, considering this. "Matias, is this a first date?"

He gave me an odd look. "Uh, yeah?"

"Dude, you have a golden opportunity to impress her, and you're passing it up?" I chided him, trying not to lay it on too thick. "If you show up in this truck, and tell her, 'Yeah, sorry about this, my little brother borrowed the truck earlier and backed it into a pole. He's promised to fix it, its all good, but talk about timing, right?' Not only do you have a conversation starter, but it shows you're generous and forgiving of mistakes, which will score major brownie points with her."

Matias blinked at me, then looked at Oron, who appeared very hopeful at this logic. Screwing his face up, Matias leaned in a little and asked sotto voce, "Will that seriously work?"

"I guarantee it," I promised without a speck of guilt anywhere in me. "Just be casual about it, don't make it obvious you're aiming for her good side."

Matias still wasn't entirely happy, but he saw a light at the end of the tunnel and his ire was more or less forgotten at this point. Stabbing a finger at Oron, he warned him, "You've got two weeks to find a shop to fix it. And if you drive it again, I'll have you by the neck."

Oron made some superstitious gesture I didn't recognize and swore faithfully, "I'll make sure it looks brand new. And I won't, swear I won't."

Satisfied, Matias gave me a considering look. "I think I see why Barrett wanted to keep you, now. You're not bad for a vampire."

I took that as the thanks it was obviously meant to be and smiled back. "You're welcome. Oron, did you at least get your tire fixed?"

Sheepish all over again, he shook his head, black hair swaying with the quick movement. "No."

"Then fetch the tire, stick it in my trunk. I'll take you to the tire place down the street and get it fixed. If we move quickly, maybe both of you will make your dates tonight, yeah?"

Seeing my point, they started moving. Matias even got into the bed of the truck and rolled the tire out for Oron, showing more forgiveness. The truck tire was rather large, but fortunately my CR-V's trunk could handle five bodies if needed, and we managed to get it inside without too much trouble. I stole a moment to put the folders and laptop properly inside Barrett's house, on the dining room table, before hopping into my car and driving both werewolf and tire toward the store.

"Thanks for that." Oron was young and prone to mistakes, but he looked far happier now that the worst of it was over. "You're right, Barrett would lose his shit to see us fighting. It would have made a bad day worse."

"Lots of bad things happening today?" I asked him, slowing at the stop sign before turning right.

"Yeah. Freaking comedy of errors. Makes me worry about the date tonight." He looked morose thinking about his future date. More likely, he was so nervous about the date, he wasn't paying proper attention to anything else.

"Naw, think of it this way: Because you got all of your bad luck out of the way now, your date will go awesome tonight."

He gave me a sideways look but brightened a little, teeth flashing against dark olive skin. "You think?"

"Isn't that usually how it goes? Have you screwed up at least three things today?"

"Uh, yeah, exactly three."

"Then you're set. Bad luck always comes in threes." I was so full of it, seriously. But he had this wounded puppy air about him, and I wanted to pull him out of his slump if I could.

We kept chatting as we hit the tire store, got it fixed—turned out it was a slow leak in the tube—and then returned. He was in better spirits by the time we made it back to his house. I helped him change it out, as he was now running late and already had to text her to tell her he'd be another thirty minutes. He hit the shower as I finished it up, put the tools away, and turned to find Barrett standing right beside the car, a faint smile on his face. I jumped, as I hadn't realized he was there. "Dammit, Barrett, make noise when you walk. My soul just tried to leave my body. What are you, a ninja?"

My reaction amused him, his eyes crinkling up at the corners, but he wasn't to be deterred. "Good work, Arbitrator."

I gave him a flat, unamused look. "Now, who told you?"

"Ria FaceTimed me so I could watch and listen to the whole conversation. Sound carries well out here."

"Noted, Alpha," I drawled, still irritated. All my hard work for nothing.

More seriously, he continued, "Thank you. I don't want fights breaking out, but there's a lot of dominant personalities, and werewolves are more...prone to physical reaction, shall we say. It takes a cooler head to intervene, and I don't have many of those in the pack. I'm just surprised they let you do it."

"Me too." I wasn't even sure why and shrugged ignorance. "I've only been with you guys, what, three days?"

"I think its more important than you realize." There was a weighing, considering way in how he looked at me. "A werewolf will only listen to someone he considers dominant, and Matias is one of the higher ups in the pack."

Wait. What? "I'm dominant compared to them?"

"That's how they reacted. They listened, after all. As I said, its very interesting." His tone made it good-interesting, not bad-interesting. "I guess we'll see how this plays out, but that's a question for a different night. For now, did you eat yet?"

"Barrett, I *can* feed myself. I'm a responsible adult and everything."

He came forward just enough to put an arm around my shoulders, physically steering me back toward the house.

"I'm curious. Do you ever feel like your body's check engine light has been on and you're still driving it like 'nah, it'll be fine'?"

It was hard to follow the thread because being tucked up against him, so cozy like this, made my lizard brain purr in contentment. I really wanted to burrow in and hibernate for a few decades. I summoned concentration from somewhere in order to answer. "Excuse you, I do try to take care of myself."

"Uh-huh. So you did remember to eat lunch?" He quirked a brow at me like he already knew the answer.

I opened my mouth on a retort and then snapped it shut again. Dammit, he had me there.

"Like I said. Ignoring the check engine light. It's fine, I have a Marissa, and I know how to use her. She's already got someone waiting for you." He pressed a quick affectionate kiss against my forehead and my slow-moving heart flip-flopped in response.

Dammit, this not-flirting flirting was going to kill me long before anything else did.

# 7

I went to work on Monday morning with firm plans to do some shopping afterward. All of my slacks were now tight, my jeans were snug enough to act like a corset, and I was literally down to two pairs loose enough I could still do the button up. I'd gained fifteen pounds over the weekend, an insane amount, but I supposed being on the brink of starving and then eating a solid twelve meals in a row would do that to you. Marissa was pleased as punched, and Barrett was openly relieved. I was ecstatic. It was so, so nice to wake up, have a lovely and filling breakfast, and know I wouldn't be starving the entire day while trying to focus on work. I even had plans to meet someone for lunch.

Of course the change in me was noticeable. My mirror plainly told me that. I didn't have a sunken look to my face anymore, like a skeleton with skin pulled tight over the bones. I had a bit of a healthy glow to me, too, less grey skin and more naturally pale. I knew the minute I walked into my office, the women I worked with would notice the difference. Sure enough, I barely went two feet inside when Ashlee, our receptionist, looked up with a general hello that stuttered to a stop on her lips.

Ashlee's bright pink lips let out a low whistle as she looked me up and down, taking off her square-shaped glasses in order to give me a better study. "Jesse. Wow, you look so much better than you did on Thursday. Emily, come see!"

From the other end of the hallway, our other attorney (and my boss) came bustling out on her platformed heels, jean skirt swaying as she walked quickly toward us, putting a pen behind her ear. Her slate grey eyes gave me a once-over, and she did the same sort of double take as Ashlee had. "Wow, Jesse! You look like you actually have weight on you now."

Fortunately, I'd already come up with a plausible response to this. "Met with a nutritionist Thursday after work, and she figured out why I reacted so poorly to all foods. Turns out I'm allergic to the chemicals most foods are processed in. She got me started on a new diet, and as you can see, it's working. I gained fifteen pounds over the weekend."

Both of these women were friends as well as coworkers—as much as I could have human friends—so it didn't surprise me when Emily drew me in for a firm hug, which I returned because hugs. Hugs were always good. "Honey, I'm so glad. We were worried, it looked like you were literally wasting away. It worried me when you called out Friday. What chemicals exactly?"

"Preservatives," I answered, drawing back as I went with the story Marissa had helped me concoct. This apparently actually was a real thing, so if they googled it, they'd find evidence to corroborate my story. "Hence why eating for me was so hit and miss. It entirely depended on the food's freshness."

"I'm glad you figured it out. This nutritionist must be very good."

"Expert in her field, in my opinion," I answered truthfully. "I'll be meeting her for lunch everyday to check in, at least for the next several weeks. We want to make sure I don't regress."

"Of course," Ashlee agreed promptly, as if this was just common sense. "Keep us updated. Although you'll have to go shopping soon, if you're going to gain weight so quickly."

"Hopefully it tapers off as I catch back up to my normal weight, whatever that's supposed to be. Otherwise, I'll be Baby Beluga." I grinned, happy they were so obviously pleased for me. I'd once thought it would be easy to pick up and move if I had to, but I would miss these two women who often went out of their way to make my day brighter. "Oh, before I forget, I met a contractor on Friday too. A friend of my nutritionist. He just moved his company down here, and I have a stack of cards to give out to anyone who needs work done. I saw some of his work, and he's good."

"Sure, hand them here," Ashlee said, reaching out a hand.

We all went to our own offices after that, settling into the workday, with me stepping out at lunch to snack on Marissa. I really had to come up with a good term for that. It was so awkward, even in my own head. I wondered what vampires normally called it?

I had a lot to do, so the day went quickly, and Marissa came around to pick me up precisely at quitting time. I climbed into her sporty red Charger and requested, "You mind if we go to the mall? I need to buy a few clothes to tide me over for the next week."

She gave me a quick nod even as she reversed out of the space. "Of course. I'm not surprised you're having trouble with your clothes now. I'm not sure what weight you'll hit, but I think you'll steadily gain weight over the next month, so I wouldn't buy much today. You'll change sizes again by the end of the week at the rate you're going."

"Yeah, I figured as much." Belatedly, I realized I never had gotten a clear idea of boundaries. "Uh, the mall is safe for us to go into, right?"

"There's a few neutral zones in the city," she assured me, eyes on the road. "The mall is one of them. Any church is neutral. Hospitals, not that anyone but the witches can go in there without getting some raised eyebrows. Government buildings."

"So the places that everyone needs access to," I summarized, mostly to myself. That did make sense. It would cause constant tension, otherwise, as people needed certain things to function in society, and being cut off from it would be asking for fights to break out. "Got it."

"Jesse." Marissa chewed on her bottom lip, taking the red lipstick off in the process, studying me from the corner of her eye. "While I have you like this, I need to ask you something."

This was going to be a whopper of a question, I could tell. "All right."

"I heard about what you did, how you intervened between Matias and Oron. Why did you do it?"

"I didn't want a fight to break out," I answered slowly, not sure what I was being accused of. Was I being accused? "And Oron shoved Matias, so it looked like it was about to get physical."

She chewed a little harder on her lip but didn't respond.

"Marissa, Barrett was perfectly okay with how I handled the situation."

"No, I know," she answered quickly, focusing on the road as the light turned green. "That's not it. Well, that's partially it. I'm a little worried about you getting in over your head, honestly, as your strength isn't restored yet. They could have seriously hurt you. But aside from that, it's...odd...to all of us that they acknowledged you and backed down."

I regarded her profile steadily, trying to hear what she didn't say. "I have this feeling I've disturbed the pecking order."

She snorted a laugh, shooting me a quick smile. "That's it exactly. When Barrett invited you to stay, we thought of you more like a guest, but you're actively engaging with the pack in ways we didn't expect. Apparently, most of the pack are choosing to defer to you. Even they can't explain to me why, as you're not doing any posturing or trying to assert authority. But they all acknowledge you're in the upper ranks, although they're not sure why. Instinctively, they just react to you that way."

I had the feeling I was either stepping on toes or she was afraid I would. "For that matter, I'm not sure where I stand with all of you. I'm not a pack leader, not a lieutenant like you are, and I'm not sure if I'll ever have the right to be."

"Typically, this sort of thing sorts itself out whenever a new wolf joins us. And of course, any child born into the pack naturally finds their own place as they grow up with us. You're an exception to the norm. I fully expect it to work itself out, things always do, but I wanted to get your take on it."

The mall came into sight, and she changed lanes to make the turn. I knew we didn't have more than a few minutes of privacy to finish this conversation, and I wanted to reassure her, as she was trying to be tactful. "Really, I'm only interested in protecting the pack and supporting Barrett's stance on things. I'll only interfere if I feel like it's necessary."

"Like last night?"

"Like last night," I confirmed.

The mall at this time of the evening didn't have a lot of visitors, so she found a parking space relatively close to the entrance. However, she didn't immediately climb out, although she unbuckled her seat belt to face me more directly. "All right. I think that's a good stance to take, but I have one more thing to talk to you about. There's a few people who think you're seducing Barrett."

My brain temporarily went offline as it tried to process this and failed. "Come again?"

"Yes, I found it amusing as well," Marissa replied, a wicked grin curving her mouth up. "To my eyes, it's exactly the opposite."

Reboot failed. (R)etry (A)bort?

Marissa cackled. "You should see the look on your face."

Yeah, I bet it was a good one. I felt like someone had taken a two-by-four and smacked me in the back of the head. Barrett was trying to seduce me? How?! Or...maybe...a lot of little behaviors were suddenly adding up in my head, things I'd chalked up to habits amongst weres. "W-Wait just minute. So that maneuver he does, where he kind of swoops in on you and puts an arm around you and snugs you in—"

"Doesn't do it to anyone else," she confirmed, still laughing.

"And that other thing, where he catches the back of your head and leans in to whisper against your ear—"

"I have literally never seen him do it before you."

I kind of already knew the answer, but my mouth was on a roll and asked anyway. "And him always standing or leaning into my personal space?"

"Now that he does do with others. It's kinda a wolf thing, as we don't know what personal space is, but you'll notice he's usually in *your* personal space and not anyone else's. Also, I have literally never seen him so protective of another person, ever. Do you know he called me just to see if you ate?" she tacked on, rolling her eyes in despair.

My mouth fished for words, a response of some kind, but brain was still offline and couldn't supply them. Ria had teased me about being exactly her brother's type, but the man acted like a mother cat with a new kitten half the time, so he hadn't been giving me the right signals for me to pick up on. Or maybe he had, but it was in wolf-ese. Cultural gap, much? This thrilled me, honestly, because I'd never dated a man as good as Barrett, but at the same time, it made me nervous as hell. I wasn't blind. If I dated Barrett, it would be just like dating a single dad with two hundred kids. Actually, that was a good point. "Marissa. Correct me if I'm wrong, but doesn't Barrett need, like, another alpha? A female alpha, I mean?"

My question got her laughing all over again. "Is that what you thought?"

"I literally know nothing about werewolves aside from what I learned over the weekend. Help a brother out, here," I growled at her. "Hollywood obviously can't be trusted. Can he or can he not have a male partner?"

"He totally can," she answered, wiping tears of mirth from her eyes. So glad I amused her. "You're right on the alpha part, at least. His partner is his stand-in if he's absent from the pack for whatever reason, so he can't have a doormat for a spouse."

Okay, so I was half right. I wasn't entirely sure how I felt about this information.

"So you *are* interested. Right?"

Craaaap. I might have given too much away with my line of inquiry. I carefully looked elsewhere, fingers knotting together, a nervous tic that surely gave me away. "I'm pretty sure you'd have to be blind and six feet under to not see the man's appeal. Hold on, that's why you were asking what my intentions were earlier."

"You're quick," she said in approval, finally opening her car door. Inquisition over now that she had her answers, eh?

I quickly got out as well, leaving my briefcase in the car, and she locked the doors behind us. In two quick steps, I caught up with her, demanding in a low voice, "But seriously, can he even pick me? I'm a vampire. That's got to be against the rules."

"You're unprecedented," Marissa pointed out, all unruffled and logical now that she had her answers. "A vampire literally has never chosen to live with werewolves before now, much less shown interest in dating one of us. No rules to break. And personally, I'm relieved to see Barrett showing interest in *somebody*. I'd begun to think there was something up, that's how long his dry spell has been."

I kept pace with her, thinking this over. It had to be ludicrously difficult to date someone in his position, though. If he dated someone inside the pack, it could be seen as favoritism and cause conflict. Outside of it, pack politics likely would come into it at some point. And it would take guts to date someone like him, knowing the responsibility that came with it. Frankly, this was the part I was unnerved about. Did I have that kind of leadership ability in me?

"It really made him happy to see you in action with Matias and Oron," Marissa added idly, as if reading my mind. "It showed you had the ability to calm down two irate wolves and solve their problem without it turning physical. Not many have that skill."

So to Barrett, I'd already shown I had the skills to be an alpha? Yikes. I felt...let's go with happy. Sure. I felt happy... but also scared, nervous, flustered, and a few other dozen emotions.

We hit the mall entrance and stepped inside the cool air conditioning. It felt blissful compared to the beating heat outside despite being early fall. The map to the mall stood in front of us, planters with greenery on either side, and a food court stretched out along the very wide hallway. I got the general impression of the place, but my attention zeroed in on the lanky man sitting on the bench about twenty feet away. He was on the phone as we walked in, but he looked up sharply as we passed through the doors. I got one good whiff of him and froze for a split second before instinct put me between him and Marissa, physically blocking his path to her.

Witch.

I could feel my muscles quiver, urging me to run, instincts clamoring. For a moment, I could only smell the heady scent of magic, and it brought up all sorts of bad memories. It damn near made me nauseous under the onslaught of smells, to the point I regretted my lunch and wanted to hurl.

More than anything, I wanted to run, but I couldn't. I couldn't leave Marissa alone with him. Who knew what he'd do to her? I couldn't have that on my conscience.

I wanted to run, though. Oh so badly.

"Uhhh, call you back, man," the young witch said slowly, then hung up before spreading both hands to the side in a deliberately nonaggressive move.

Marissa put both hands gently on my shoulders, whispering to me, "I told you, this is a neutral zone."

"I believe you. Problem is, he reeks of magic." I could never forget the smell, not in a million years—like acid, molten heat, and the rising energy of a mother storm all combined in one. The odor clung to him like a second skin.

"Wow, you can smell it?" Witch scratched his three-day-old stubble, dark eyes sharp on me. He looked like the quintessential next-door neighbor, harmless and a little scruffy, handsome in his own way. I didn't trust appearances. "You've got an extra sensitive sniffer."

"No. Just had a bad experience once."

"Ouch. One of us, eh? Well, not us, we're not into the dark magic stuff. White witches, that's us." He stood and approached, but when I didn't drop my guard, he paused. "Yeah, okay, let me explain why I'm here. A new store just opened up in the mall yesterday, some new age thing, only there's some problematic inventory. They've got some incense candles in there with spells engraved into the wax. The humans just think it's cool shit, probably, but the spells are working 'cause they're activated by fire. They're revealing spells, to make matters worse."

"Revealing spells, as in...?" Marissa trailed off, studying the guy over my shoulder, although she had to prop herself onto her toes to manage it.

"As in, all of us are no longer behind the magic curtain, yeah. I mean, it'll show my magic in a visible aura, but for weres? It'll force a shift to your furry forms in a snap." Witch grimaced. "I was reporting it when you walked in. It's seriously not a good idea to be in here today, at least not if you're going toward the east section of the mall. I swear to you, it's not one of us who opened the store, and if we'd known about it before now, we would have stopped it from coming in."

I strangely believed him. My flight or fight had died down enough my body had stopped trying to jerk me into motion. I should still remain cautious, but if he stood here candidly talking about the issue, in a mall, I felt like he might be trustworthy? The last time I'd met a witch, I'd been ambushed in a less than public place, so the experience alone was worlds different.

I think Marissa trusted him too, as she came around to stand next to me, giving me a pointed look. "I'm Marissa, from Walker Pack. This is Jesse, also from Walker."

"Anthony, from Blue Moon Coven. Wow, a vampire and a werewolf in the same territory? Seriously? Did Oscar have a hernia when he found out?"

If he disliked Oscar, I was even more inclined to give him the benefit of the doubt. "Just about. He wanted me to join them. I didn't like his methods."

"Dude, you're smart to avoid him. He's a douchebag." Tapping a finger to his mouth, Anthony offered, "In the spirit of goodwill, let me escort you guys through here. Just for today. I'll deflect the revealing spell. Yeah? We don't want trouble here, and we'd prefer to stay on the Walker Pack's good side."

I didn't really care for the idea, but then again, I only knew about witches through  my single awful experience. Marissa, who knew more than I did about witches, didn't flinch and even looked like she was considering following him.

"Maybe tell me how you joined the pack while we shop?" Anthony added in with unabashed curiosity.

Blowing out a breath, I considered all the angles, but we were in a public mall. In daylight. I didn't think he'd really try something here. Still, just in case...I pulled out my phone and called up Barrett. He answered in two rings. "Barrett. I'm at the mall with Marissa, and there's a bit of a situation here."

"*Dangerous?*" he asked, and I swear to you, I could just hear him going for his car keys.

"Potentially, but before you start driving over here like a bat out of hell, listen." I filled him in, all the facts, and he did listen without asking a single question. "I'm inclined to do some shopping and scope out the situation. Anthony of Blue Moon Coven has offered to escort us as a goodwill gesture until his people can sort out the problem. What do you want us to do?"

He hesitated audibly for a good second. "*Play this by ear. Try going farther in. If you think it's too risky, thank the man for his offer and pull out. If you're not home in an hour, I'm coming in after you, so be quick.*"

"I'll call once we're free of the mall, or text you," I promised. I didn't want the man to either charge in here or grow an ulcer in worry.

"*I'll warn everyone to steer clear of the mall until it's resolved. Get Anthony's number if you can. We have no way of communicating with his coven right now, which is obviously not good.*"

"Roger that. Sit tight, I'll let you know," I said, then ended the call. "He wants us to go in a little farther, see how bad it is. If it's all right, I'll shop quick. Anthony, we have no way of communicating with anyone in your coven. Do you mind if we have at least your number?"

He nodded instantly, nonchalant. "Sure. Me and our head witch, how about that?"

"All right. You can have mine and Barrett's in return." This situation made me uneasy, but everyone was being so logical about it all that I felt foolish for even thinking of arguing. Still, I was cautious as we exchanged numbers, and I had my guard up as we walked farther into the mall. The magic smell grew stronger, nearly burning my nostril hairs, and once we reached the four-way intersection in the middle of the mall, even Marissa made a face.

"All right, I smell it now," she muttered, nose scrunched up like she'd put her face square into a poopy diaper. "Yikes, that's a very distinctive and unpleasant stench."

"To you guys, maybe. Smells good to a human nose." Anthony shrugged. "Where we going, man?"

"Men's department store. JCPenney's works." I just needed cheap clothes that looked decent for work and something I could lounge in. It didn't have to be expensive.

Fortunately, the shop I needed was to the left, away from the problematic store. Marissa charmed a tape measure away from a sales associate, measured my waist, and we went directly to a sales rack. As we shopped, Marissa casually told Anthony the abridged version of how I came into the pack, and he asked more than a few questions. I still wasn't really comfortable with him and let her do the talking while I picked stuff out and tried them on. I went a size bigger, figuring they would last a little longer. I'd need a belt to keep them up for the next few days, but it shouldn't be a problem.

I bought five work shirts, three pairs of slacks, two pairs of jeans, and some underwear. On second thought, maybe some loose workout clothes to sleep in?

Marissa appeared at my side, studied the selection, and went for a pair of joggers and a matching jacket. "You'll need something for the full moon this weekend."

"Come again?" Was that supposed to make sense?

"Full moon," she repeated, like this was obvious. Snapping her fingers, she realized aloud, "Crap, I don't think we told you. On the night of a full moon, we go out in the desert and run together, just cut loose. Gives everyone a chance to work some of the energy off. It's a pack thing."

"Ah. Yeah, in that case, I definitely want something with a jacket. Gets cold at night. Maybe something warmer than this one, though." I didn't care if it matched the joggers. Okay, maybe I did care if it coordinated, but that wasn't the same thing.

Anthony, trying to be helpful, picked up something neon green with leopard print. "What about this? It's warmer."

"Uh, no."

"He's gay," Marissa explained to Anthony seriously. "He won't wear it."

"Marissa, it's not because I'm gay. It's because I have eyes." Pointing a finger at the jacket, I informed them sarcastically, "And my eyes will flee from their sockets if I put that on."

"How about this pretty teal jacket? It works well with your coloring." She pulled out a fleece-lined windbreaker and dangled it in front of me.

"Yes, all right, fine." I pulled it on, just to check the fit, and it was long enough in the arms and had some extra width to it, so I shrugged and added it to the pile. "Okay, I think we're good for now. How long has it been?"

"Thirty minutes. You better call him."

"He said an hour," I reminded her.

Marissa just looked at me. "Jesse. Do us all a favor and call him. Remember what I said earlier?"

Yeaaah, okay, she might have a point there. I pulled my cell out and called even as we made our way toward the nearest register. He once again answered on the second ring, and I could hear the unease in his voice. "*Jesse, I'm in the parking lot. Which store are you at?*"

Catching my eye, Marissa mouthed, *See*?

Yes, so I did. "Listen to me, you mother hen," I retorted, exasperated with him. "You said an hour. I said don't come unless I'm not out by then. It has been *half an hour.*"

"*But you said it reeks of magic in there.*"

"Barrett. I swear on the next full moon, if you come in here, I will hijack your phone and change your autocorrect so that it says 'nyoom' whenever you try to type anything. I will make every messaging app you have useless. Do you understand me?"

For a moment, just a second, my words penetrated his worry and he actually snickered. "*That is probably the most creative threat I've ever been handed.*"

We'd reached the counter, and I put all the clothes down and smiled at the cashier before replying. "I'm paying now, and I'll be out in five minutes. Hold your horses, worrywart."

"*All right, I'm out here on standby. I found Marissa's car, so I'm parked next to it.*"

"Okay. See you in a bit." As the lady rang me up, I asked Marissa in an undertone, "He will get better, right? It's just my current state making him like this?"

"When you're back to full health, he'll ease off. It's that and us in conflict with Oscar's people that's put him on high alert," she guaranteed. It would have been vastly more reassuring if she hadn't added, "I think."

Sighing, I paid, because what was I supposed to say to that?

Anthony wisely didn't say anything, but he gave us more than a few looks, as if we'd said interesting things he wasn't quite sure what to make of. He'd been perfectly pleasant so far, helpful, and the longer I was around him, the more I felt like he could potentially be an okay guy. By the time we made it out of the store, once again heading through the mall and to the parking lot, I thought perhaps I'd done him a disservice. I didn't trust him fully, but I unbent enough to explain, "I was in bad shape when the Walker Pack found me. Marissa told you how they fed me? I'm only now getting my full strength and weight back thanks to them, hence my need for new clothes."

"I wondered," he answered, his tone and expression careful, clearly not wanting to antagonize me. "No offense, but you don't look healthy to me. And if your alpha is keeping such a careful eye on you, it means there's a problem."

"Yeah." I didn't know what else to say and left it at that.

"Oscar's man attacked him on sight, despite him not doing anything to warrant it, which is also why we're protective of him," Marissa pitched in from my other side. She hefted one of the bags higher to ride over her shoulder as she spoke. "Oscar has now supposedly gotten it through their heads to not hurt him, but you never know."

"Dude, sounds like you've had a rough time recently. And I hate to ask, but gotta know because you didn't like the sight of me. Have our people given you a rough time too?"

Honesty forced me to admit, "No. I haven't met anyone from your coven aside from you. A bad history with witches in general makes me wary. Sorry if I offended you, Anthony. I'm cautious because of what happened in the past."

"Fair enough, man. I don't blame you." He stopped at the four-way, hesitating. "Should I meet your alpha? Problem is, I've got people coming to help me with the store situation, and I expect them any second."

"Go handle them," Marissa encouraged. "We can make a more formal meet and greet later, since we have each other's numbers."

Anthony looked relieved, which made me wonder if the store situation worried him more than he'd let on. "Sure. Let's do that. Nice meeting both of you." With a wave, he took himself off.

"Well, this has been a very educational shopping trip," Marissa noted wryly as we beelined our way for the front door. "I can't wait to get away from this stench. I'm glad you're a fast shopper."

"Normally I'm not, but all things considered, I sped things up." I inhaled a deep breath as we hit the doors, letting the cleansing air sweep through my nose with relief. So much better. I caught sight of Barrett leaning against the bed of his truck, but as we came out, he immediately straightened and speed walked to meet us part way.

He looked like he'd just gotten off a job, his jeans dusty, his black T-shirt hugging his trim body in all the right ways. Walking toward me like this, backlit by the setting sun, he really did look like a model for some kind of construction magazine. Did construction people have magazines?

I digressed.

I looked at this man with the new realization he'd been flirting the past few days and felt my heart go pitter-patter. He was gorgeous, even covered in dust, and I was apparently pretty far gone because all I could think about as he walked to me was how much I would love to get my hands on him. I felt more aware of him on a physical level, too. I could feel the tingly start up, that hyperactive sensitivity people experience when they're next to someone they liked. Shit, what was I supposed to do about this?

"All right?" he asked, eyes sweeping over both of us as he stepped in close, his hand taking the shopping bag from me and switching it to the other side, giving him room to come in even closer.

"We're good," Marissa assured him, giving me a significant look.

Yes, Marissa, I was not oblivious to the fact he'd stepped on my shadow and had a hand on the small of my back. Now that I knew how to read his cues better, his body language told me everything I needed to know. I just wasn't sure why he hesitated in making a move. Granted, I hadn't flirted back at any point, so maybe he was unaware of my feelings on the matter? Dang it, think about this later.

"We have phone numbers, and Anthony swears they'll tackle the store today, although he didn't know how long it will take. So the mall will be off-limits for now."

"You don't want to be in there anyway, the stench is horrendous." Making a face, Marissa handed me the other shopping bag. "Here, see you at home."

"Sure." I loved how she assumed Barrett wouldn't let me ride home with her. Despite my briefcase still being in her car.

We loaded the bags in the back of the King Cab, and I had to hop up a little to get in. Barrett's black F-250 was clearly a work vehicle, as the outside had the classic smudges and dings of a work truck, but he tried to keep it clean on the inside. A little dirt, but nothing bad. I had more crap in my car than he did. I buckled in automatically as he started the engine.

"You were good with the witch? He wasn't sketchy at all?" Barrett asked as he backed up.

"No, he's quite an easygoing guy. I eventually felt bad for being so on guard with him. I don't think he's like the witches I met back then. I have no idea if the rest of his coven is like him, though. I know they're a very secretive bunch, as Ria's been trying to track them down for months and she's not had much luck. She said something about them not having much of an online presence."

"Yeah, that's what she told me as well." His eyes darted to me for another look, this one more thoughtful, and I could see the tension unwind in him slowly now that he had me safely away from any danger.

It made me want to try something, push a little and see how it changed matters. Marissa had opened so many possibilities to me, but I didn't want to sit back and wait to see how right she was. Werewolves did a lot with scent, which gave me an idea. I leaned in next to his shoulder and inhaled deeply. "Ah, much better. You smell like sunshine and warm rocks."

"Shit," he rasped, abruptly pulling over into a random parking lot. He threw the truck into Park as he jerked his seat belt off.

Umm. I hadn't quite expected this reaction. Had I just tapped into werewolf instincts somehow? I had no chance to act—he was on me in the next second, one hand catching my head and keeping me still as his mouth fastened on mine, teeth tugging on my bottom lip. Lust slammed through me so fast I went dizzy with it.

He pulled back just as quickly as he'd engaged, his damned worried expression back. "Jesse. Jesse, you know you can tell me no, right?"

"Why the fuck would I tell you no?" I growled, not sure whether to hit him or pull him back in.

"Just checking." Barrett wasted not another second and dove back in, a touch rushed, but sweeter this time.

I slid my arms around him, leaning in, kissing him back and loving every second of this. My body tingled, active and alive in a way I'd not felt in years, and I loved the way he kissed me—like he couldn't stand to do anything else. My hand swept up and into his hair, playing in the thickness of it, even as my tongue tangled with his, a hot glide that made me wish I was in my new pants. I needed the room. Or maybe no pants. I was a fan of no pants.

He pulled back gradually, lingering in a soft kiss, then stopped to look at me as we caught our breath. I didn't let go of him. I had no intention of doing so until I had it straight just what the hell we were doing.

Barrett took all questions out of my hands by asking seriously, "I'd like to date you. Can we?"

"After a kiss that hot? We better be fucking dating," I informed him, exasperated, and he lit up like a Christmas tree. "And for the record, werewolf social cues confuse me. I literally had no idea you were flirting until today, when Marissa straightened me out."

"Ah." He blinked, considered that, and shrugged. "I owe her, then. I couldn't get a read on you, so I wasn't sure if you were interested."

"I'm not dead, Barrett." I was back to being exasperated, but with a smile firmly in place. "So yes, I'm interested."

"You're really inflating an already dangerously inflated ego," he told me, grinning. For once, there was no obvious worry, no other thing he was thinking about, just pure happiness as he looked back at me. It was there in his eyes, a light all of its own, and I was proud as punch for putting it there.

I hadn't made out in a car since my teenage years, but an important fact reared its head. "Your house is still full of people, isn't it?"

"Probably, yeah."

"Then get back here," I ordered, snapping my seat belt off. "I'm not done with you yet."

# 8

Don't ask me how they knew. Scent? The pleased grin on Barrett's face? My own baffled, happy expression? Whatever it was, it took the pack exactly two seconds to figure it out and then we were inundated on all sides. I didn't even fully clear the foyer before I had questions lobbed at me.

"When did this happen?"

"Wait, can it happen?"

"Barrett, does this mean he's now leadership too?"

"It's about time you two got your acts together!"

"What do you want us to do about explaining this to the kids?"

Barrett looked both put upon but also edgy, his eyes constantly darting to me. I think he feared I'd reconsider, now that the heat of the moment had cooled, and I realized just how much responsibility came with dating him. As if I hadn't realized it already. I rolled my eyes and said loudly, "Everyone to the living room. Sit!"

They obeyed, although I heard Luis complain, "He's treating us like dogs."

"I'm treating you like the nosy person you are," I retorted to his back, "and if you want answers, then sit."

Flashing me a grin, he made a show of picking a patch of floor and obediently sitting on a cushion.

I went to the fireplace, the only clear space, and looked out over the sea of faces. It probably wasn't more than a hundred people, not even the full pack, but it certainly felt like more. I'd never been one for public speeches, but apparently I needed to learn and learn fast. Barrett stood at my side, regarding me curiously, and I let him because I needed to make a few things clear to both him and the rest of the pack. "All right. In order. Yes, we're dating. It's been a whole hour since we started, so obviously we don't have everything figured out. I am not your alpha"—not yet?—"and I'll take what authority Barrett decides is appropriate to give me at this stage."

People blinked at this, then immediately turned to Barrett.

My newly minted boyfriend smiled back at them. "He's got good common sense, so if there's a situation, feel free to come to him, just like you'd come to any of us. And if any of you try to scare him away, I'll bite your tails off, so bear that in mind."

This got more than a few laughs and some wolf whistles. No pun intended. I put up with it patiently, as I felt sure their intense interest would die down eventually. I found it interesting he trusted me to this degree, though. He'd barely seen anything of me, comparatively speaking, but he knew he could trust my judgment? I'd definitely ask him questions later in private. "You can tell the kids the truth, that we're dating. For that matter, if any vampire comes within range demanding answers, you can tell them we're dating. I don't care if they know or not. Now, questions?"

"Who made the first move?" Of course Luis asked this.

"He did," Barrett answered promptly.

I eyed him sideways. Did it count as a move if I didn't know I was making one? Sure, okay, let's go with that.

Marissa carefully asked, "Barrett, you still okay with the rest of us feeding him?"

Ah? Why would it be an issue?

One look at Barrett's face and it clearly was an issue. He hesitated strongly, eyes searching my face for the answer. I wasn't quite sure what was going on here. I assumed it had something to do with territory, but that was a guess. I did not think it a good idea for Barrett to solely be the one feeding me, despite a werewolf's healing powers, as that would drain him dangerously.

Maybe he came to the same conclusion. Maybe he realized he was being ridiculous. Either way, he blew out a breath and assured her, "It's fine."

I wrapped my hand around his, rewarding him a little for being sensible despite what his instincts told him. He laced our fingers together, smiling at me softly.

"Damn, they're cute together." Ria sighed happily.

Biting back a chuckle, I winked at her. "All right, any other questions?"

"Changing subjects," Luis said, lifting a hand in the crowd. "But what's the situation with the mall?"

"We're still waiting on the local witches to deal with it and call me back," Barrett answered with a one shoulder shrug. "I don't expect that to be fast on their end, they'll need to hop through some legal hoops to get it all sorted. Avoid the mall for now. I'll notify everyone once its clear. Okay, that's it, dismissed!"

People didn't really disperse, but Barrett led me out of the living room. He took me up the stairs and into his bedroom, which, granted, was probably the only private space in this house right now. He closed the door behind us but didn't sit, just turned to study me intensely.

"You really surprise me sometimes."

"How so?"

"You've got such a quiet, unassuming air about you, and then you do something like announce to an entire pack of werewolves you're dating their alpha and they better not give you trouble about it. Most people would have been quaking in their shoes."

Oh. Was I supposed to have been nervous? "Well, but, the pack's family, right? Why would I be nervous about telling my family I'm dating someone?"

A slow grin took over his face and he leaned in to kiss me softly. "No reason. No reason at all."

"Barrett, be honest with me, as part of what happened downstairs alarms me. Is the feeding thing an issue?"

His smile morphed into a grimace. "It's territory. In case you haven't picked it up yet, we wolves are highly territorial. Especially with our significant others, we don't have any chill. I recognize, though, they're acting for your good. I can't be upset about that. I also can't be the only one to feed you. It would dangerously weaken me, and for what? Pride? It's a stupid reason. I won't fall into the trap."

Barrett's common sense was correct on all points. Still, I could tell this rubbed him wrong instinctually. I twined my arms around his neck and thought fast. "How about this? Every time I feed from someone, I'll come to you and kiss it better."

"Kiss my pride better?" Barrett's eyes crinkled up in a silent laugh. "My ego's not that fragile."

"So no kisses?"

"Now hold on, I didn't say that."

Silly man. I raised up on tiptoes to kiss him softly, glad I could tease him, even about this. He kissed me back with affectionate, light kisses I thoroughly enjoyed.

He pulled back and murmured, "Stay with me tonight? We can just sleep, if you'd like."

I appreciated that he asked. Consent was sexy. Was I willing to lie next to this man and just sleep? No way in hell. "Barrett, don't ask the impossible of me. If we're in the same bed, I'm jumping you."

This got him laughing. "You really make me feel like I'm sexy and irresistible."

"Uh...you are sexy and irresistible."

"Dangerous territory you're running into there, honey. My willpower is not that strong." The mother hen look edged back into his expression. "Um. All things considered, maybe Hector should check you out before we get physical?"

This freakin'...ugh.

I didn't know what came over me—I swear I was not the impatient type—but some kind of instinct made me grab him by the waist and lightly toss him onto his bed. Barrett was so surprised he didn't even try to dodge me, just went with it, landing with a bounce.

Then he busted out laughing.

"If I can throw you," I informed him archly, "then I can certainly do *other* things. No checkup required."

Barrett continued to laugh as he came up on elbows. "Sold. Get over here."

Didn't have to tell me twice.

# 9

After a bit more time of making out on the bed, Barrett coaxed me into the shower—something about white noise to drown out sounds for the many werewolves with keen hearing downstairs—and admittedly, it didn't take much coaxing. Shower, bed, didn't matter to me. I just wanted hands on him right now.

I'd get him on the bed later tonight when I knew the house was empty.

Clothes kind of went every which way, my focus more on getting him naked than hitting a hamper. It could be, in part, because I'd not had a lover in six years, but it wasn't solely that. I suspect Barrett could always turn me on in a second flat. I kissed him over and over, hungry for him in a way I'd never been for anyone. Barrett barely had the spare attention to get the water heating up and us into the shower, his main focus on kissing me back.

Finally, though, we were surrounded by tile and water, his naked skin pressed against mine. I had to stand on tiptoes to kiss him —damn height difference—but it was such a joy to do so. I kissed him, then slanted my mouth sideways, trailing over a cheek, down the column of his throat. He smelled *so divine*, like the most delicious morsel I'd ever come across. I could smell his blood, too, richer and thicker than it had been before, the sound of his heartbeat like a drum under my fingertips.

Those large, warm hands trailed down to my ass even as he tipped his head farther to the side, giving me access to the column of his neck.

"You hungry, *mi cielo*?"

I grazed my teeth against his skin, just enough to not break through. Felt him shudder from head to toe, and his shiver had everything to do with pleasure and anticipation.

"I'm not," I denied, my own voice sounding strangely hoarse in my ears, "but I am? You just smell so good."

"Nibble, then."

I didn't want this to be about a feeding, though. I wanted sex. He just smelled really, really good, and my teeth ached with the need to pierce skin, and his blood called like a siren's song, and...and...shit.

My teeth were in his skin before I knew what I was doing and the *taste* of him, god. Like ambrosia that coated the tongue, the most satisfying thing I'd ever eaten. Some part of my rational mind wondered why Barrett tasted so much better now than he had previously, but I was too busy enjoying it to really question it.

He was filling, too, much more than usual. I wanted to eat more, but my poor stomach protested the idea. I licked him clean and felt him vibrate in my arms, nearly shaking with need.

Oh, he was rock hard against my stomach. Seemed he'd enjoyed that very much too. I gathered his dick up in my palm, stroked him, watched behind hooded eyes as he threw his head back. He was so incredibly sexy like this, so easy to please and sensitive to every touch.

I trailed my mouth down, finding a nipple, laving at it with my tongue.

"Hngh!" Barrett jerked against me, thrusting up into my hand.

Look at him, so far gone he was on the edge of exploding altogether.

In a move almost too fast to track, he seized my thighs with both hands and whirled, moving us both until it was my back pinned against the tiles. He captured my mouth— tongue diving in and tangling with mine—and tasted his own blood no doubt. It didn't turn him off; he groaned into the kiss, pushing my legs apart so he could thrust his dick up against mine.

If this man got any sexier, I might melt in a puddle of pure lust. I caught both of our dicks in my hands, caging them so he could thrust against me. I felt the drive, the heat, even as Barrett dominated me. My instincts craved the dominance, the feeling of his body caging mine, his hot skin against my own making me feel as if I were on fire. The coolness of the tile was in such sharp contrast against the heat pouring from his body, I felt nearly insane with it.

My mouth broke from his on a cry, head thrown back as I came harder than I ever had in my life. He jerked once, twice against me and came as well, shuddering, his groan muted against my shoulder.

My god. I knew sex with him would be good—just kissing turned my brain off—but I didn't know it would be literally *mind-blowing*. Brain's offline, may have left building, try again later.

The water cooled by the time he lifted his head. I wasn't sure who held up who, our arms still snug around each other, not leaving enough room for even water to pass between us. Those beautiful eyes snagged mine, and he seemed to share the joy of good sex as well as the disbelief.

"Jesse, you okay?"

"My knees might be rubber," I admitted. "No faith I can keep my balance if you let go."

"I'm in slightly better shape. All right, let's get out. I want to talk about this."

About...what? The fact we have insane chemistry? Or that feeding from him during sex was a completely different experience?

Well, probably both.

With Barrett's slow-moving, cautious pace, we shut the shower off and got out. My legs really didn't want to support me, but I somehow managed to stay upright. He insisted on drying me off with a towel—which was cute, if unnecessary— before picking me up and carrying me to the bed. I still felt a little warm, so I didn't even try to get under the covers. The very second Barrett deemed himself dry enough, he snuggled into the bed with me, propped up on one elbow.

"So, um." We had to start this talk off somewhere, but I had a feeling I was about to make a hash of it. "That was a lot more than I'd bargained for."

"Same." His fingers gently swept hair back from my eyes, the touch a lover's caress. "I don't mind admitting it was the best sex I've ever had."

Oh good, he felt the same way about it. "Me too."

"I certainly don't mind a repeat," he assured me with a rich leer. "Although apparently I need to get lube in here."

"Please and thank you." The idea of him—over me, in me, fucking me while I bit him—flashed through my mind. The image alone almost got me hard again for him. Damn, must try that next.

"Before we start exploring the many, many fun positions awaiting us, I must ask about something else."

For some reason, I felt a little embarrassed. "Me biting you, you mean."

"Absolutely not upset about it," he assured me gently. "Rather the contrary, but I'm also very confused right now. You've bitten me without any sex involved and it felt pleasant, so I would've offered again for the nice sensation. This time? It was incredibly intense and just as good as the sex."

I blinked up at him. Uh, come again? This made no sense. "Why was it different?"

"I do not know. Now, I think someone mentioned there's a lot of rumors about vampires and their orgies?"

"Uh...yeah. On the first feeding with you guys."

"We dismissed it as tall tales then, but apparently, there's truth to it. I reacted very strongly to you in the shower."

"Something about pheromones in the sex making the difference?" I had no other theory to offer. Then again, I didn't understand vampire chemistry to begin with. It didn't make any scientific sense, for that matter. "But why?"

"Maybe? I had an unmistakable reaction, though, more in line with what I've heard through rumors."

"Huh." I literally wasn't sure what to do about that. "I, uh, don't want to have sex with anyone else though."

"I'll be very mad if you do."

I figured that would be the case, possessive man that he was. "What I'm saying is, I'm not willing to test this on others to prove a theory."

"I'm very much on the same page." Barrett leaned in to kiss me softly. "What do you think about me reaching out to another clan for answers?"

"Uh. Not a vampire clan, I hope?"

"Not anyone local," he assured me with a brief grin. "We know better after that shit show. No, someone else entirely. There's a single clan I know of who's on the East Coast and very mixed in nature. It's an oddball out of all the territories, actually, as they have everything from dwarves to vampires to werewolves in it. It's only referred to as a 'clan' since the leader is a vampire, despite the mix. But I'm friends with one of the werewolves, Dunham. If I ask, he'll at least put me in contact with one of the vampires. Maybe we can wrangle them visiting for a week or so?"

If he trusted these guys enough to invite them into his territory, that said a lot to me. "I would love a week to just pick their brains."

"Honestly, at this point, I feel we must at least ask. There's so much about you we don't know or understand. It's a disservice if I don't try."

He really would move the world for me, if I needed it moved. My heart softened at the realization, and I found myself smiling up at him without any conscious decision to do so. "Then let's ask."

"You won't feel unnerved being around another vampire?"

"I don't think so. It's not like they'll have an agenda to push, right? I won't be in any danger from them."

"All right, if you're sure, I'll message him tomorrow." His eyes traveled over me from head to toe, and I could see him lose the thread. "How, uh, tired are you?"

"Not that tired," I assured him on a laugh. "But don't you need lube for what you're thinking? I'm sure someone somewhere in this pack has some."

Barrett scrambled for the end of the bed. "Do not move. I mean that. I will be back here in three minutes, tops."

Knowing how fast a werewolf could run when motivated... "It'll take you three whole minutes?"

"One minute," he amended, already with boxers on and a foot out the door. He stabbed a finger at me. "Do not move."

Then *whoosh*, he was gone.

I cackled as I heard him run down the stairs. This man of mine sure did make me feel sexy.

Now, what was the most provocative pose I could put myself into? I wanted him to lose his mind the second he returned.

I was, admittedly, a little shit sometimes.

# 10

I woke up the next morning feeling the pleasant soreness that came from lots of sex.

Turned out werewolves had *amazing* stamina and the libido of a horny rabbit. Please note I absolutely was not complaining.

Barrett had kissed my forehead earlier, saying something about needing to make some calls, but I'd been too sleepy to do more than grunt at him. He'd tucked me back in and let me sleep a bit longer, but now I was awake and missing him. I also had work this morning, it being a Tuesday, so it wasn't like I could just stay in bed anyway.

I was all set to roll out of bed when my hand brushed against something tucked underneath my pillow. Wait, what was this? Pulling the object free, I attempted to process what I now held.

A sunflower.

Wait, had Barrett left a flower under my pillow? Shit. Could this man get any sweeter?

Grinning ear to ear, I placed the flower on the nightstand and headed for a quick shower. After pulling on work clothes, I fetched my sunflower and wandered downstairs, wanting to put it in a proper vase. Halfway down the stairs, I noticed it was strangely quiet, and I wasn't sure why. Normally this house was packed to the rafters.

Or was everyone giving us a bit of space this morning? Awww, cute of them, if that was the case.

Barrett sat on the couch for once, phone in one hand and a laptop balanced on his knee. He looked up as I came downstairs, giving me the smile I'd kinda already fallen for.

"There you are. Hungry?"

"I nibbled on you most of the night," I pointed out dryly before kissing his cheek. "Thank you for the flower. I love it."

"You're welcome. It's *el regalo de almohada.*"

"A whatsit?" I had no idea what he'd just said, but clearly I still had a lot to learn about my lover yet.

"'Pillow gift' is the easiest translation. In my culture, we like to leave little gifts for our lovers, as a token of our affection. I felt that was best."

The saying went that Italian lovers were best, but I guess that went for Hispanic men, too, because damn, Barrett had game. I leaned in and kissed him fully this time, lingering a moment before pulling away. "You are too sweet."

"For you, always. You're sure you're not hungry?"

"I'm not, I promise. What are you doing?"

For once, he let the feeding-me-thing go and waved me in closer. "Waiting for a call from the friend I mentioned. I texted him, and he said to give him a few minutes and he'd call me. Also setting up the last details of this weekend."

I gave him this blank *huh?* face. "Whatsit?"

"Full moon is this weekend," he reminded me. "We generally bring lots of snacks and beer because shifting takes calories."

"Ohhhh." I hadn't realized it was that big of an event for them. Like, I had, but I hadn't. "So we're going shopping for snacks at some point today?"

"I really need to, yeah."

"I'm game." A shopping date sounded fun to me.

"Good. Then after we talk to Dunham—" Barrett's phone rang in his hand. "Speak of the devil. Hey, Dunham."

"*Hey, yer fine self,*" a deep, rather gravelly voice responded. "*It's been a dog's age since we talked last. How ye be?*"

"A lot better than the last time we talked," Barrett answered with a laugh. "The move went well. We've settled into new homes, business has been going well, and I've acquired a boyfriend."

"*Ha! Well, damn fine, then. Life canna be more grand than that.*"

"No, indeed. How are you, man?"

"*Oh, I be fine. Also had quite a few changes here in me clan but all positive, all for the better. I'm recently married, in fact, to the most bonnie lass I ever laid eyes on.*"

"Congratulations! That's amazing to hear."

"*Thank ye, I'm quite chuffed about it. What's this yer ringin' me about, anyway? Ye adoptin' vampires, now?*"

"Yes and no. I'll put you on speaker so he can chime in. Dunham, meet Jesse."

"*A fine hello to ye, sir.*"

"Hi yourself," I said, leaning a little against Barrett's arm just to get more comfortable.

Barrett picked up the explanation smoothly. "As I texted you, he was changed by a rogue, and we invited him into the pack after we realized the vampires in this area can't be trusted for shit. But it leaves us guessing at how to help him. He's gone six years without properly eating, and it shows. But we don't know the rules and regs on that, or what's best to maintain his health, or…anything, really."

"*Hmm, seems to me there be too much to try and explain over a phone, as well. Will ye be all right with a visit, then?*"

I blinked, not expecting his offer.

"I'd love to have you visit." Barrett didn't even pause to think about it. "But are they all right coming?"

"*Oh, I be sure they will. If not me clan head, then maybe one of the others, such as me wife. She's newly turned, though, not sure how many answers she can give ye. All the vampires be sleeping right now, but they're due to wake in a few hours. I'll run this properly by them then. Now, one other thing I can offer while we wait for them to awaken be this: We acquired a hacker a few years ago.*"

Say what, now?

Barrett's brows shot into his hairline. "A hacker?"

*"Name's K. He be a trip. His brother—who be a thief, by the by—and me clan head go way, way back. Got into mischief in their younger years, ye know how it goes. When we had a patch of trouble up here, Glenn called Eidolon in, and we met the family in the process. Lovely people, truly lovely. K, knowing we'll need fresh IDs every decade or two, has offered to help us manage it."*

I gave my boyfriend a pleading look. I mean, I was trying, but those systems were made to prevent the very thing I was attempting to do. And last I'd heard from Ria, she was still banging her head against a firewall.

Barrett chuckled a little. "That takes no thought on my part. I'd be happy to pull him into my pack too. We're on the verge of being in trouble ourselves with licenses and such, so we definitely need the help."

*"I'll pass it along, then. Dinna be surprised if ye get a call from an untraceable number."*

"Noted. I assume you're coming along too for a visit?"

*"I wouldna miss it for the world,"* Dunham promised with enthusiasm. *"In fact, I think I can get there in time for the full moon. That'd be a blast, running along with all of ye. Might drive so I can bring me dogs."*

"They're welcome," Barrett assured him. "Always more fun when you can bring dogs along on a run."

*"I'll do that, then."*

"What about your new wife?"

*"Ah, well, she still be working night shifts at hospital. A nurse, y'know, likely can't take off that easily. I'll ring off, expect an answer sometime later this afternoon."*

"Will do. Thanks, man." Barrett ended the call with a satisfied smile stretching across his face. "I knew Dunham would help. He's seriously a good friend."

He'd told me something about the man last night, between bouts of hot sex, so I didn't inquire further about him. Just one thing raised questions. "Dogs?"

"Oh, we love dogs," Barrett said with a wicked grin. "We can communicate freely with them, after all. They speak in very simple, broken sentences, but they do talk. We lost most of our dogs due to old age shortly before we moved here, and I requested no one adopt or buy until we got settled into our new territory. Really, we're settled enough, so I should encourage people to go adopt again."

This was all news to me, but it did make me wistful. "My parents used to raise collies when I was a kid."

Barrett's eyes turned affectionate. "You can have a dog too, if you'd like."

"It's really, really tempting. Let's get me a bit more sorted out first."

"Fair enough."

"Want to go shopping for snacks after work?"

"You read my mind." Barrett closed his laptop and set it aside. "We need to get all the things, plus a few staples like toilet paper."

I figured. Also, it was a nice way to kill some time and have Barrett one-on-one, which was something of a trick. I'd take advantage while I could. First, though, sadly—work.

Couldn't someone else come adult for me?

After work, we had everything under the sun loaded into Barrett's truck, which took forever to unload into the house. I collapsed onto the couch once we were done, feet up on the armrest, not interested in doing anything else for several hours.

Barrett came back into the room with the phone pressed to his ear, smiling. "Do you mind if I pause and tell him?"

Oh no, I had to pay attention again, didn't I? Dammit. With a sigh, I sat back up.

"Ross is on the phone," Barrett explained as he came to sit down next to me, phone in hand.

Oh, the vampire who was clan head. Or married into it, I guess. "Hi, Ross, I'm Jesse."

"*Hello, Jesse,*" a mild tenor voice answered. "*Welcome to the crazy world of the supernatural.*"

I snorted a laugh. "Yeah, crazy about covers it."

"*Until you have to rescue a member from the pound, you have not reached peak insanity, I promise you.*"

I blinked. Uh, he didn't sound like he was kidding?

"Are you serious?"

"*It's a thing with werewolves. They do not always choose the best moment or location to play dog, let's put it that way. Anyway, I understand you are only recently a part of the pack, and there's much about being a vampire you do not know about. What do you know?*"

"Uh...we need blood for survival and being too long in the sun is ouchy."

There was a pregnant beat.

Then a long sigh. "*I now understand why your boyfriend is calling. There's much you need to learn. I do not think a phone call here and there will cut it, either. I only recently turned myself—*"

Oh, really? Huh, it would be interesting to meet a new vampire like myself.

"*—so I know from experience, there's a lot you must change or adapt to. Barrett assures me we're welcome to come and visit, and I'm inclined to agree it's a good thing. How about we start our drive out later tonight or so?*"

"I'd love to have you on hand for questions." I meant every word. "Is it all right?"

"*Of course. I wouldn't mind a little getaway from my clan's craziness, truth tell, so I started preparations earlier. Having an honest excuse to get away for a week is a gift horse I'm not looking in the mouth.*"

All right, I liked Ross. I could tell already this man was going to be a friend. "Then please do come."

"*We're already there. Just text me an address. For now, eat when you're hungry. Don't force it, just eat when you feel rumbly in your tumbly.*"

I gave my boyfriend a speaking look. "I can do that."

Barrett didn't even pretend to be abashed. "I'll have the guest rooms ready when you get here. Is it just you, Glenn, and Dunham coming?"

"*Most likely, but I'll give you a firm number here in the next hour. For now, assume us three. Also, Dunham mentioned something about you guys possibly adopting dogs soon?*"

"Right. We lost all of ours before we moved down here."

"*Jesse, I hate to say it, but you're going to be the voice of reason here. Do not, I repeat, DO NOT let the werewolves go into the shelter without you. They will adopt all the dogs if there's no voice of reason to rein them in.*"

Surely he was kidding? Only, he didn't sound like he was.

Barrett laughed. "Don't scare him. We've never emptied out a pound. Anyway, we're looking forward to you coming. See you soon, Ross."

"*Sure, bye.*"

I didn't trust Barrett's airy dismissal and eyed him suspiciously. "You've never emptied out a pound, huh?"

"Naw, not like his clan did."

Oh god, Ross was speaking from *experience*?

"The last time we went to adopt dogs, four of them were on hold awaiting their families, and at least three weren't adoptable for health reasons," Barrett continued thoughtfully. "So we left some behind."

In other words, if given the chance, he totally would have emptied out the pound.

Thank you, Ross, your forewarning came very timely indeed. Whether or not I could prevent the adoption of an entire pound, well, that remained to be seen.

# 11

Ross, Dunham, Glenn, and at least six dogs arrived three days later. I'd taken off about two hours early from work in order to be at the house when they arrived. It was a bit chaotic at first, greeting everyone, turning the dogs loose in the yard, and all. Still, I was relieved to see them. I really, truly needed more guidance.

Dunham was clearly an old friend of the pack because after he said hello to me, he basically disappeared with his dogs. I heard a lot of barking, howling, and play noises from the other yards, so presumably people were having a ball with their new friends.

Once people were more settled in, I ended up at the dining room table with Ross and Glenn, not exactly by plan, but damn, what a view. They were truly a beautiful couple to look at. Glenn very much had that Irish charm, with freckled skin and beautiful burnished terra-cotta hair he'd styled over to one side. Ross was his opposite in looks, with taupe skin and amazing apple-green eyes. I felt like I sat opposite of a power couple, and they likely were if they managed a whole clan of various supernats.

Glenn's words had a slight, charming burr to them as he spoke. "Jesse, I do not mean offense at all, but you don't look well fed to me. I know feeding was hit and miss before you came to the pack, but this much?"

I sighed, kinda slumping in on myself for a second. "Prior to meeting the Walker Pack, I kinda just made it up as I went along. I didn't know how to get access to blood without assaulting people, which I wasn't okay with doing. I made do with coconut water—"

Both of them winced.

"—which, as you know, does and doesn't work."

"Vegan vampires," Ross muttered with something like despair. "Gah."

"When Barrett and his pack met me, the first thing they offered was blood. Believe it or not, this is an improvement. I've gained thirty pounds since coming into the pack."

Glenn winced again. "I can see why they are so worried for you. All right, how much are you eating now?"

"More or less three meals a day." I sensed my boyfriend coming into the room and gave him a slight smirk. "Plus snacks."

Barrett smirked back at me as he dropped into the chair next to mine, slinging an arm to rest over the back of my chair. "We are feeding him, Glenn, I swear. He was just in an emaciated state when we first met him."

Ross did a full-body shudder. "I hesitate to think of how bad you were before you met them, then. All right, once you're in a healthy state, you won't need to feed on a daily basis. It's more like monthly."

"We sometimes eat more often than that because of"— Glenn's eyebrows waggled mischievously—"snacks, but generally speaking, a month is fine and will keep you in a healthy state. The longer you live, the longer you can go without eating. Something about vampiric chemistry ages well. My mother, for instance, generally eats every three months or so. But she's nearly five hundred years old."

I had my phone with me and whipped it out so I could take notes. "So once a month is my goal, then. How much do I need to regain, weight wise, before I can slow it down to once a month?"

Glenn shook his head. "No, don't use weight to measure by. I know American culture is obsessed with weight, but it's not a good standard. Every body type is different. I've adopted vampires before who were in dire straits, and it took time for their full health to return. Let your appetite guide you. If you feel like only eating once that day, then eat once. If you're hungrier, eat twice. Use your body's signals to judge by."

This seemed like good advice. That said... "Those other vampires, how long did it take for them to regain their health?"

"I think the worst of the lot was Helen, but even she wasn't as bad as you. It took nearly a year, if memory serves."

Ouch, I was the worst he'd seen? Well, that was disheartening.

Barrett stirred, also looking really unhappy hearing this. "But he's not in danger, right?"

"No, no, he should recover fine," Glenn hastily reassured him. Then looked back at me. "The wonderful thing about vampires is the ability to bounce back from anything short of a beheading. Our nature is very hardy. You'll recover fine from this without any ill effects. Just don't rush your healing. Let your body have the nutrients it needs."

I nodded along, relieved at finally receiving some solid advice from another vamp. "I mean, I've basically been eating nothing but blood since the Walkers found me, so I think I'm okay there. But that's really good to know, thank you."

Ross kept giving me this suspicious look I hadn't done anything to deserve. I don't think?

"Jesse," he spoke slowly, suspicions weighing at every word, "something you said over the phone before we left bothers me. You said the sun is ouchy. Are you actually going out and about during the day?"

"Um...am I not supposed to?"

He let his head flop into one hand. "So glad we came. No, you're not supposed to."

"But he can handle being in the sunlight," Barrett objected. "I've seen him do it."

"He can, yes, but *handling* it is all he's doing." Ross rubbed his jaw before looking back up at us, clearly unnerved. "A lot of the myths surrounding vampires are just that, myths. But there's some elements of truth to them. Sunlight, for instance. You need to treat yourself like you're anemic, if that makes sense. Your body can't process direct sunlight well, and it's taxing upon your system."

"It's why we sleep until mid to late afternoon," Glenn threw in, also giving me an unnerved look. "We just can't handle sunlight well, and it's draining to us. Especially when you're in this state of recovery, I would highly suggest avoiding sunlight completely. It'll slow your recovery a great deal."

"Oh." I hadn't realized this at all, but come to think of it, a lot of the outdoor activities I used to do, I'd stopped doing. I'd chalked it up to not having any energy for them because of my poor diet, but this made sense too. "I have a full-time job, though?"

"Office?" Ross checked.

"Yeah, I'm a real estate and tax lawyer."

"Ohhh." Ross gave me an approving nod. "That's a good skill set for your pack. That said, if you're in an office setting, it's not as bad. Still, once you quit—and at some point you'll need to—I would suggest doing something like a work-from-home situation. And work nights. Mornings are forever going to be a challenge and sunlight's a no."

"Got it." Well, that was a worry for future me. Current me was happy to keep my job. I didn't want to let go of a well-paying job just yet.

"That's the basics of what you need to know. We'll cover things more in-depth tomorrow, as it's a long conversation, and there's something else I need clarified right now." Glenn folded his hands together and looked at me seriously. "I heard the short version of how you were turned and why. I have two questions for you. First, this black coven, were they dealt with?"

"I, uh, don't know? Honestly, I wasn't interested in going back and finding out what happened to them. I escaped and called it good."

"This perturbs me. I want to verify what happened to them. I'll give the clans in that area a heads-up of what happened and when, let them deal with their own matters. I'm not interested in being involved, but a courtesy call is not amiss. We clan heads try to look out for each other when it comes to mutual threats, at least. But keep in mind, not all clans are good," Glenn said wryly. "Much like all men are not good."

"Yeah…you got me there. What's your second question?"

"The vampire who turned you, what was his name? We try to hunt down the rogues, or invite them into a clan if we can."

Made sense to me. "I wouldn't hunt him down, he was a good guy in a really awful situation. He got me out, after all. His name's Huxley."

Both Ross and Glenn went stock-still. The kind of still only a vampire could pull off. Then their eyes darted to each other, and I could tell the name rang a bell.

"Do you know him?" Barrett blurted out in surprise.

"I…might? Huxley's not a common name." Glenn lifted a hand to show a height that was a bit shorter than mine. "About this tall, inky black hair, high brow?"

"My god," I breathed, feeling like I was having a Twilight Zone moment. "Yeah, that's him exactly. Said he's originally from England, but, like, southern England. Although, he sounds like he's from Virginia?"

"That's him precisely." Ross sat back with a huff, astonishment written all over his face. "Jesse, he's not a rogue. He's very much a member of a clan. He's from a vampire clan in Salem, in fact. I've met this man several times."

Ever feel like someone yanked the rug out from under you, then kicked the back of your knee for good measure? My chest felt tight as I processed Ross's words because, well, if Huxley was part of a clan, then…then all the assumptions I'd made about him were defunct.

"Can you call him?" I blurted out. I had no idea where those words came from, as I hadn't meant to say them, but frankly, a large part of me yearned to speak to Huxley. I wanted answers, if nothing else.

"Oh, we're calling him," Barrett rumbled. My boyfriend was *pissed*. "For leaving you as he did, he has much to answer for, and he might not stay breathing if he gives me the wrong answers."

I, uh, shit. I didn't even know how to feel about this. A man who I'd thought completely abandoned me six years ago was suddenly within reach. I felt like I needed a lie down and maybe a stiff drink for this knowledge to really settle.

Did they make Bloody Marys with actual blood? Not asking for a friend.

# 12

Ross called Huxley right there on the spot, waiting impatiently for it to ring. It took a few rings before the call picked up.

A voice I hadn't heard in six years, sounding just as rough around the edges as back then, answered with a note of trepidation. *"Ross? What's broken?"*

Ross didn't seem to think the question was weird. Which made me wonder just how rowdy his clan was. "Huxley, did you turn a young man about six years ago in order to escape a black witch coven?"

There was a startled intake of breath. *"I did! How the hell do you know about this?"*

"I'm talking to the man you turned right now—"

*"YOU FOUND JESSE?!"* The question was full of demand and also ringing with excitement and joy.

I felt nonplussed about this reaction because first of all, I wasn't missing. Secondly, he sounded like a parent who'd lost a child, which was strange. I mean, I knew vampires were protective of their progeny and all, that had been explained to me, but Huxley hadn't really chosen me as his "child." His reaction now made no sense to me. More than anything, I felt hurt by all of this. He was the one who abandoned me, right? So why was he acting excited just hearing about me? Was it wrong of me to feel a little resentful, maybe betrayed?

"I found him, all right." Ross kept one eye on me, the other on my hovering boyfriend. "He's in Arizona. Huxley, I'll put you on the phone with him, but— Oh, VidChat now? Okay, thanks for the warning."

"*Turn the camera around,*" Huxley ordered impatiently. "*I don't want to see you.*"

"Fuck you too." Ross didn't seem bothered, more amused, as he flipped the phone about and handed it to me.

I took it with some trepidation, straightening the phone so I could more easily see the speaker. Huxley truly hadn't changed one whit in appearance, except he looked healthier. He'd looked like he'd survived WWIII the last time I'd seen him. He also wore this mile-wide smile, and I think if he'd been here in person, he'd have glommed on and not let go.

His eyes roved over me and his dark brows tightened in an unhappy line. "*Jess, my god. Are you all right?*"

"I'm, uh, actually much better than I was before." I felt a hand land on my shoulder and reached up to cover it, giving Barrett a quick shaky smile. "I was just adopted into a werewolf pack, you see. Huxley, what *happened*? Where did you go?"

"*No, I don't see—and we'll come back to that—but...*" His shoulders slumped, reddened eyes falling from mine. "*I understand if you're angry with me. I didn't give you all the tools you needed to survive. I abandoned you, but you must believe I didn't do so intentionally. I heard the damn witches coming early that last morning. I left to draw them away from you and then ended up wounded. I had to go to ground for several days to recover. By the time I got back to your building, you were gone. I couldn't track you.*"

My breath caught at his words, and I stared at him in puzzlement. "You...meant to come back to me?"

"*Of course. You're my child. I realize this might be strange for you, to think of me as a parent, but I made you.*"

"Wait. Wait a sec, you're not making any sense. You made me so we could both survive. You didn't do it by choice."

"*Perhaps not in the traditional sense, but the moment I placed my fangs on you, I took responsibility for you. I never intended to leave you on your own. I never wanted that. You accepted the change with good grace, despite the deplorable conditions we were in. You showed restraint and intelligence. You'd make any parent proud. Of course I wanted to keep you with me."*

I was perfectly stunned by this admission. I'd never once thought he might want me with him. That he thought of me as his own. My mouth opened and closed several times, but I had no words to offer. I could feel tears burning in my eyes because, honestly, I'd not felt the love of a parent in years. My own biological father was estranged from me, mostly through his own choices, and I'd not had contact with him in years. To suddenly have parental love and concern again impacted me more than words could express.

I honestly thought being adopted by the pack, being loved by Barrett, would be enough to heal all the scars on my heart. But hearing I'd never been abandoned by Huxley healed another wound in one fell swoop. I felt a surge of love so strong the memory of my heartbreak became distant, easier to forget. I still wanted to hear all the details of him, learn properly about this man, but I now had *time*. A precious gift once stolen from me, suddenly given back.

*"I'm so, so sorry."* Huxley shook his head, no doubt remembering those early days we had together. I certainly was in this moment. *"Believe me that I've looked for you, but once you left the area, I couldn't pick up your trail."*

"I changed everything," I whispered, and felt Barrett step in closer, like he wanted to both comfort and protect. "I moved, changed my phone number, changed jobs—everything. I was paranoid at first about the black witches finding me again, and I wanted out. Plus people were giving me weird looks because of all the physical changes I'd gone through, and it seemed wiser to just leave."

*"I feared that's what you'd done. I had no way of tracking you afterward."* He ran a hand roughshod through his black hair, visibly upset. *"I consoled myself by thinking that at least you'd left the area before the witches could get to you. But seeing you like this, I can't... Jesse, how bad is your condition?"*

"I promise you it's improving."

Barrett leaned in over my shoulder to growl, "He damn near starved before we found him. He was subsisting on coconut water."

I saw Huxley wince.

"We've been feeding him multiple times a day since we adopted him. He is recovering." I heard a hint of pride in Barrett's voice. He was very much not happy with Huxley, that was clear too. "What did you plan to do once you found him?"

Huxley seemed to realize the only thing saving him right this second was Barrett's inability to punch him through a screen. "*As any other vampire would, I would have taken him in as my child. I do have a clan who would welcome him but*"—his eyes darted to me and he looked rueful—"*I have a feeling suggesting so would shorten my lifespan.*"

"Significantly," Barrett agreed, not even masking his anger.

Huxley just huffed, too amused to be surprised. "*Jesse, what do you want from me now? Whatever you want, be it answers or a proper relationship with me, I'm more than willing to give.*"

You'd think I'd need to sleep on it when offered a father-slash-son relationship. Strangely, though, I didn't. I knew the answer instinctively and my mouth hijacked my brain before I could overthink it. "I want a relationship with you."

Huxley's expression melted into a smile that was joy unleashed. "*I want that, too. You're the first child—the only child—I ever made, you know.*"

"I...seriously?"

"*It's why being separated from you was even more heartbreaking. My only child, and I couldn't even point in your direction. It's kept me up more than a few days and nights. Jesse, if you want a father, you have one. I'll come immediately to you, all you must do is say the word.*"

I didn't need to think too hard on that, either. I wanted to see him. I wanted to have the relationship I should have always had with him. We'd trauma bonded, if nothing else, but I wanted to see if we could actually be family to each other, too. Greedy? I wasn't sure, but I wanted to give it a try.

"I do, but I have to warn you, I'm living in a rather large werewolf pack right now."

Huxley waved this off. *"I think even better of them for helping you. I want the full story of how it came to be when I see you. Assuming your very protective werewolf boyfriend will let me anywhere near you."*

He wasn't exactly kidding and we all knew it. Barrett was so protective right now that FedEx would consider a hug from him to be bubble wrapped.

Barrett spoke up first. "If you want to come here and see him, I'll allow it."

Eh?

"*Huh?*" Huxley perked right up, eyes alight. *"If you mean that, I'll be on the next plane. Ah, Jess, run this by your alpha first—"*

I pointed to Barrett. "He's the alpha."

*"Oh. Then I apparently have permission. Thank you. I'm coming immediately."* Huxley lunged for something and was back in a second with pen and a pad of paper. *"Cell? Address?"*

I rattled both off, relieved we finally had each other's contact info. I just had one question. "Huxley. That coven... it's gone, right?"

*"It is now. I had some of my clan meet me down there and we wiped it out."* Huxley shot me a wink. *"So you can sleep peacefully."*

"I'm relieved." I really was. I wasn't in any danger after moving across the country, but still, I felt relieved evil like that was terminated and didn't linger in the world.

"I'll be on the next flight out," Huxley promised again, nearly vibrating in place, he was so eager to move. *"Jess? Just don't disappear on me again."*

Silly man. "I wouldn't dream of it."

# 13

I felt beyond happy right now. Like, over the moon. It was such a relief to finally have Huxley in my life again. I had to wonder if vampire instincts were at play here, or if I felt this way because I'd lost all connection with my birth parents. My father had never been hands on with me or even really affectionate, which only got worse after my parents' divorce, so I didn't know how a father should act. But Huxley was so excited about me, I had a feeling he'd be the father figure I'd wanted for most of my life.

"Excuse us a few minutes." Barrett pulled me up from the table and guided me out to the back patio.

I had no idea why he was doing this and leaving our guests alone, so I gave him a look askance.

He put both hands on my shoulders, eyes concerned. "Checking in. How are you feeling?"

I didn't know what kind of karma I had to get a boyfriend with a high EQ, but damn, I must have saved a country in a previous life. I gave him a hug for his thoughtfulness alone.

"I'm overwhelmed in the best of ways."

"Yeah?"

His tone encouraged me to talk about it, so I did. "My mother died years before I was even turned, and we weren't close when she passed. My father hasn't ever been one, if that makes sense. He wasn't really fond of kids, and I haven't spoken to him in over a decade. I don't even know where he is. The second I was done with high school, it was like he felt he'd done his parental duty, and then he took a job overseas and I lost all communication with him. Even before I met

Huxley, we were basically low contact. So having this option of having a father again, it's like being offered treasure. I'm really, super happy about this."

"Then I'm happy for you."

"Is it really all right for him to be here?"

"Sure. I personally don't have anything against vampires—"

I snorted at that because, obviously.

"—it's just that most vampires I've met have been absolute pricks. So long as he's not a douchecanoe, he's more than welcome here."

"Cool. I just don't want you to suffer in silence if something goes wrong, okay? I want this connection, but not if Huxley is an asshole to you."

"All right, fair enough. You don't know the man super well at this point, so we'll see how this plays out. But so long as he's good to you, he's good to me."

"Got it." I snuggled in a little more for a second. "Thank you."

"No need to thank me for this. Honestly, having him here for a while will relieve me because at least he'll help you recover once Glenn and Ross leave. And he can teach you how to properly vamp."

"Yeah, truly, I'm happy for that alone."

We just stood there for a moment, arms wrapped around each other, and I felt it again—a sense of being in absolutely the right place. It wasn't just that I felt welcomed and accepted here in the Walker Pack. It was the fact I felt absolutely loved when I was in Barrett's arms. Safe, too. Not just in a physical sense, but an emotional one. I could say anything to this man and not be judged for it—something priceless.

Barrett gave me one last squeeze before kissing my forehead and stepping back. "Let's go back in."

"Sure."

I followed him in, finding Ross and Glenn still at the table. At some point while we were gone, Marissa had taken a seat at the head of the table. She was earnestly talking to them when we walked back in.

"—trying but he's only able to do so much. How do you guys handle this?"

"Widow or K," Ross answered.

"What are we talking about?" I resumed my seat, all ears.

"Licenses," Marissa answered with a hopeful expression. "Because our doctor needs an updated license—and so will you, eventually—so I figured I could ask how they handle it."

"Oh yes, please. That's a particular brick wall I'm tired of banging my head against. Dunham mentioned something about a hacker friend."

"We don't have anyone with specialties in the clan who requires a license, aside from my own mother, but she's very recently turned so we haven't had issue with that one yet," Ross explained, head panning back and forth as he tried to explain to all three of us at once. "But we made friends with a thief family who's been both very generous and helpful with this issue. Used to be, I did all the paperwork for people to 'die' and then be 'reborn' so they could have updated driver's licenses and such. Then I acquired K's and Widow's skills, and now they do a lot of the legwork for me."

Glenn picked up the explanation. "I'm actually friends with Eidolon. He's an amazing thief. There's no place he can't get into. When we initially met up with him, he told me they'd adopted a few kids into the family. Widow is the eldest and she's a trained hacker. K is her mentor, and he's the best hacker I've ever heard tale of. The two of them are a force to reckon with once they get going."

I was fascinated by this glimpse into the underworld and had to ask, "Are they supernatural as well?"

"As human as they come, but very accepting of us. We've done a few jobs together, in fact, the most memorable being a high wizard's mansion this past year." Glenn's expression was both rueful and nostalgic. "Ah, good times, that. Anyway, if you'd like, I can put a call in and see if I can introduce them to you. They'd likely be willing to help, for a fee."

I gave my boyfriend praying hands. "Please."

Barrett smacked a kiss against my forehead. "No problem, they're worth the price. I've seen you and my sister struggling with this for the past week. Let's solve the problem if we know people who can do it."

"I love you and will have your babies."

Barrett laughed, the sound like a rumble coming out of his chest. "You really don't want to sit for the bar again, do you?"

"I really, really do not."

"I'm calling Widow, then." So saying, Ross picked his phone up off the table and popped open a contact.

It rang a few times before there was an answer, which sounded like a very smooth, young soprano. *"Hi, Ross. What's on fire?"*

Seriously, I suspected his clan was even worse than mine about finding trouble.

"Hi, Widow. Fortunately, nothing on fire yet," he answered with a roll of his eyes. "That I know of. So, how do you feel about helping another supernatural group with licenses and paperwork?"

*"I'm always up for breaking more laws. Who am I helping?"*

"Werewolf pack this time, out here in Arizona. We're friends, and they're in a tough spot. They have both a doctor and a lawyer in house who need licenses renewed at some point, and they're not sure how to go about it. The doctor's license I understand is more a priority than the lawyer's."

Truly, mine could go another decade without an issue.

*"Hmm, haven't hacked a medical board thingy before. This should be fun. All right, I can do it, but I'd really like to be on site for the initial phase. Just so I can get a feel for what all they need, maybe teach them some tricks so you guys aren't dependent on me. After all, you'll all outlive me."*

"That's a very sad reality. How do you feel about being turned?" Ross's tone was all sass.

Widow snickered. *"You're a bad man. It's why I like you. We'll talk making me a sexy vampire queen later, let's focus on the boring shit first. I'm, hmm, somewhat in the middle of a job right now. I think it'll wrap up in a few hours, though. Let's say I'll come your direction by tomorrow morning. That work?"*

"Absolutely. Thanks for this, Widow."

*"Sure, you betcha. Shoot me an address and I'll let you know when I'm on my way. Kisses~"*

Ross ended the call and looked very satisfied. "She's seriously the best. I want to adopt that girl."

Glenn gave a full-body shudder. "I'm not risking it. I'm not pissing off a thief, a hacker, and an assassin. You'll never find my body. We'll have to seduce her into the idea first."

"Eh, it might not be too hard. Anyway." Ross gave us the smile of a very satisfied man. "Your expert help is en route. Any other problems I can solve for you?"

"Can I just keep you?" I was half joking saying this, but seriously, Ross was one of those magical beings who seemed to know all the right people and how to solve every problem. He'd solved all of my problems in an hour flat. I wanted to be like Ross. Barring that, couldn't I just keep Ross?

Glenn grinned at me like I'd said something hilarious. "You know, that's exactly why I brought him into my clan to begin with. He's able to just solve problems as they come at him. Of course, it took a gas station blowing up to convince him to enter my clan, but that's a different story."

"We've got time," Barrett pointed out. "Why don't we crack open a few beers and you can tell us about it? This sounds like a fun story to hear."

"Well, I certainly don't mind."

I absolutely didn't mind. This was a story I wanted to hear, and I had time until Huxley arrived, so why not relax and enjoy these fabulous new friends?

Huxley somehow managed to get on a red-eye flight that night. Being a natural night owl now, I was fully awake by the time his plane landed and went to pick him up at the airport. I was admittedly nervous about seeing him. What if this didn't work out smoothly like it had in my head? What if we couldn't get along on a daily basis?

What if, what if, what if.

Barrett sensed my nerves, I think, because he reached over the divide to take my hand. His grip felt comforting and settled the frogs leaping about in my stomach.

"It'll be fine. Just take it as it comes, don't try to force anything."

"Good advice." I'd do my best to take it.

The airport line wasn't long at this time of night, as few people chose to fly in for a midnight arrival, so it didn't take us long at all to pull up to the right spot. The pickup area was brightly lit, of course, it being the dead of night, but also rather deserted. I spotted Huxley without trouble, and the second Barrett had the truck stopped, I popped out to welcome him.

Huxley had a single suitcase he rolled along the sidewalk, but he abandoned it the second I was in view, swooped in, and bear-hugged me right off my feet. I startled, not expecting this, but the second I was in his embrace, I felt a huge surge of relief. Which surprised me again, as I hadn't expected that, either.

Not being able to find this man, to be with him, had eaten a hole me in I hadn't been fully aware of until Huxley was suddenly here to fill it. I felt tears burn my eyes as I hugged him back. With him here, it felt like I was suddenly complete. I had no explanation for the feeling of why, it just was.

For once, I chose not to question and simply basked.

"Son," Huxley choked out, arms steel bands around me. "God above, it's good to finally be able to hug you. But you're so thin, are you really all right?"

I pulled back a smidge to see him up close and reassure him. He did look heartier than I remembered. He wasn't a tall man at a few inches shorter than me, but his shoulders were wide and muscular, accented by the red and black plaid shirt he wore. "I really am. I'm healing now and much stronger than I was before."

"Your boyfriend said something about you subsisting on coconut water, but he was kidding...?"

I shook my head.

"Fuck. He wasn't kidding?" Huxley's head dropped for a second in despair. "But I told you how to feed!"

"You didn't teach me how to be all seductive and charming. I can't even pick up guys in a bar, okay? There's no way in hell I can convince a complete stranger to let me nom on them and keep my secret."

"Ugh. There's much I'll need to teach you. I'm glad I'm here. All right, let's go back to your house. I'm very interested in meeting your pack."

"Sure, let's go. I'll introduce you to everyone tomorrow. Most are asleep right now. Ross and Glenn are still up, though."

"I truly, truly owe them for making the connection and calling me. I'd never have found you, otherwise."

I owed them too. How I'd ever pay this back, I had no clue, but hopefully I'd be able to in the future. Right now, though, I was going to focus on Huxley and rebuilding the relationship we'd lost.

Fortunately, as a vampire, I had all the time in the world.

# 14

I stayed up rather late with Huxley, wanting to catch up, and of course Ross and Glenn hung out with us until the wee hours of the morning. It meant we all slept in very late, which felt far more natural than getting up at some ungodly hour of the morning like eight a.m.

Ross might have a point about vampires versus mornings.

Anyway, fortunately for us, Widow wasn't due until about three in the afternoon, so I was able to sleep in until well after noon before needing to trek back out to the airport to pick her up.

I wasn't sure what I'd expected for a young hacker, but a stunning young girl about eighteen years old with waist-length butterscotch brown hair, wearing skinny jeans and a shirt that said *Sasshole, Queen of Sass* was not in line with what I thought of as "dungeon hacker." Then she grinned, and I could see not only the sass, but the mischief as well.

I was going to like this girl, I could tell now.

Ross had come with me to get her from the airport, and Widow the Hacker greeted him with a hug.

"Hi, friend."

He hugged back, grinning. "Hi, trouble."

"Aww, you do know me well. I'm here for mischief and shenanigans."

"You are definitely at the right place. Let me introduce you." Ross stepped back and waved a hand between us. "Widow, this is Jesse, of Walker Pack. Jesse, Widow."

"Name's Remi, but I answer to both easily," she said with a smile and held out a pale hand.

I shook it but honestly wanted to hug her instead. "Thank you so much for coming. We're really up shit's creek here. Ria's a good hacker, she can help with a lot of this, it's just the licenses and certifications giving us grief."

"So I understand. I'll happily impart my knowledge. If we get stuck, I'll call up Uncle K. He's my mentor, and the man's forgotten more about hacking than I know."

"Fair enough. Let's get you loaded up."

She had two oversized suitcases, so I took charge of both, taking them to the trunk of my car. One of them felt definitely heavier than the other, for some reason.

"Be careful of the blue suitcase," Remi warned me. "It's got my computer in it, so it's heavy—"

I hefted it into the trunk before her words hit and just looked at her. This was heavy?

She rolled her eyes. "Vampire strength. Right. Anyway, I'll just get in the car."

Amused, I finished loading the bags and then hopped into the driver's seat. I got us underway, Remi riding shotgun with me. She looked me over from head to toe before turning her head to address Ross in the back seat.

"So you guys do auditions, huh?"

"I'm sorry?"

"Every vampire I've met has either been super hot or cute as hell. So you do auditions, right? Like, 'sorry, you're too ugly, hard pass' kind of auditions."

I snorted a laugh. "Trust me, no audition on my part. I was turned out of desperation."

"So I hear. Love to get the story, if you don't mind. I'm still adapting to the supernatural world, so I'd like to know what or who to avoid."

"Fair enough." Speaking of avoiding, I wondered how the mall fared? I hadn't heard from my witch friend, Anthony, for several days now.

My phone abruptly rang through the car's speakers. Speak of the devil. I hit *Accept*. "Hi, Anthony, what's up?"

*"Hey, man, just wanted to tell you we finally got those revealing spells taken down. It took some serious negotiations and some promises of different wares they could display that we'll make, but it's finally done. I'm walking the mall now, verifying things are cool, and I think we're good to go now."*

"I really appreciate it, man. We all need stuff."

*"I bet. Hey, any reason why Marissa texted me and said stay out of the desert this weekend?"*

"Huh? Oh, it's 'cause it's a full moon tonight. We're planning to run around in the desert as a pack."

*"Oh. Shit, yeah, I'd forgotten it was this weekend. I'll pass on that experience. I'd get pounced on for sure."*

"It's mostly the kids. They're rambunctious on a full moon and not in control of their instincts."

*"Yup, super hard pass. Thanks for the heads-up."*

"I'd rather you not be collateral damage." I laughed. "Thanks for the mall back. And let's have that boundary meeting soon, all right?"

*"For sure. I'll let you go." Click.*

Phew, finally. The mall situation really had taken Anthony's coven a while to settle.

Remi gave me a quirked brow, questions clearly over there percolating. "Mall? Revealing spell?"

"New age store with problematic merchandise. Local witch coven stepped in to take care of it. We're still trying to settle boundaries with everyone in the city. The witches are sometimes hotheaded, and recently, the vampires have been pushing for more space, so it's become this giant headache. "

She snorted. "You don't consider yourself a vampire, do you?"

"Er...not really?" Hearing her say that, it felt obvious to me. I was a vampire only on a biological level. My thought patterns and responses were all wolf. Ha, funny how that had happened.

Ross muttered something in the back that sounded like "Poor Huxley," but I ignored him.

"Well, Remi, let's introduce you to Ria. You two have lots of fun government sites to hack."

"My favorite thing," she said brightly.

Her sincerity was a little scary.

I'd asked our vampire guests if they wanted to come out into the desert running with us, but all had declined. Even Ria had stayed back with Remi, having far too much fun with girl talk and hacking, apparently. She'd promised to join in later, only wanting to hang back for an hour or so.

The rest of the pack, though, me included, very much looked forward to cutting loose tonight. It was a glorious Saturday night with no responsibilities in sight for the rest of the weekend, and I wanted to take advantage of it.

The desert wind was sharp and cool. Not cold, not yet, although it would get there around midnight. I lifted my face into it and breathed deep, appreciating the crispness of it. Sounds of rustling Buffalograss, lizards skittering over rocks, and birds chirping at each other drifted along the wind. I took them in without processing, just letting it all flow over me.

As I stood there in this barren patch of nowhere, almost two hundred people stripped off clothes and shifted into their furry forms. I supposed nudity came with the territory for werewolves, and I tried not to let it bother me. I'd get used to it, assuming I did this often enough with them. Since I wasn't shifting, I kept my clothes firmly on. I'd need them later.

When everyone had changed, they started howling at the moon and yipping at each other. I did not speak wolf but had to assume this was some sort of signal.

Barrett was not the largest of the wolves, but he still stood as tall as my shoulder even on all fours. He padded over to me, snuffling at my neck and then rubbing his head against my chest. Smiling at him, I scratched behind his ear, as he seemed to be asking for it. His fur was softer than I'd assumed it to be, and a rich dark brown, bordering on black. Or maybe the pale lighting of the moon made it seem that way. I enjoyed burying my hands in the softness. His tail wagged at the attention, but he didn't stay in the position for long. Lifting his head, he gave a loud howl.

The signal was clear. Time to run.

They didn't go full speed—we had kids with short legs in the pack, after all—but they certainly set a good clip. I ran at about half speed without strain, matching pace with Barrett. It was nice to stretch out like this. Half speed for a vampire was about the same as full speed for an Olympic runner. I couldn't really run in the city or at a gym, not like this. It would draw too much attention.

The upside to it, though, was the ability to run and run without getting winded. The desert floor wasn't smooth or level—there were little dips and rises, random outcroppings of boulders—and my pace got thrown as I cleared these obstacles. Still, navigating them and still keeping up was half the fun. I also hadn't had this kind of energy in a long time, years in fact, so it felt liberating to just *go*. The wolves had their tongues lolling out of their mouths, a sure sign of their enjoyment as they ran.

For a moment—an insane and thrilling moment—I felt incredibly liberated. I felt a connection to the people I ran with, deep inside of me, an instinctual thing I couldn't describe with words. In that instance, I gained a sense of belonging I'd never had, not since I was a small child.

We ran in a giant circle, staying within a fifteen-mile radius, and then on some signal, slowed to a halt. I didn't understand why, not until I realized it was a field of sorts. A large rectangle had been cleared out, with white painted boulders marking the boundaries at all corners. The wolves split up, some of them spectators as they sank to their bellies to watch, others lining up along the far edge of the field. One wolf—I think it was Tanner, judging from the size—stepped into the middle, tail wagging, his head down low, clearly ready to pounce.

Barrett stayed next to me, and while I had no idea what was going on, he acted like he was the referee. He let out a short yip. At his signal, the wolves flew into the field, running and trying to dodge Tanner. Tanner was quick to pounce, though, and more than a few "died" in an exaggerated manner, flopping onto their sides before dragging themselves good-naturedly toward the sidelines.

I watched this play out and thought I knew the game, although normally I saw it played in a pool. "Is this Shark and Minnows?"

Barrett gave me a deliberate nod, not taking his eyes from the players.

"Really, you play games out here? Not just run around?"

He snorted in amusement and rolled his eyes at me.

It did make sense. Running was fun, but if you were going to be out for most of the night, might as well play too. "Can I be the shark next?"

Barrett canted his head at me, clearly in question.

"I've never really tested my reflexes," I explained, anticipation kicking up a notch. "It'll be fun to see how many people I can catch."

My boyfriend thought about this for a moment before giving a very human shrug and another nod.

"Sweet."

I dove into the fray, and it was immediately apparent that while I wasn't outmatched, I had definitely met my match. Especially in Marissa. Who cheated.

Still, we went several rounds with the game, and I had a lot of fun. It didn't leave me in a sweaty exhausted mess, but I felt the exertion of trying to catch very athletic, agile werewolves.

Eventually, I came back to the sidelines and grabbed a Gatorade from the pre-arranged refreshments. Just because it felt like the appropriate reaction, even though I technically couldn't get dehydrated. Unless I was super low on blood.

Barrett shifted back to human form, quite comfortable in sitting next to me naked. Wolves apparently didn't subscribe to this whole modesty thing. It somehow suited them better than clothes did, although it took me a minute to get used to it.

"You've now spent two days with other vampires who aren't douchebags."

I had no idea where this opening statement was going, so I made a noise of agreement.

"Are you tempted to go back with them?"

It took a second to hear the insecurity underlying those words. What the hell was this man saying? Why would I be tempted? Or was this just some fear preying on him? I had a bet it was the latter.

I snagged his chin with two fingers and brought him in close enough for a lingering kiss. When our lips parted, I saw his eyes dilate with hunger. I hadn't meant to rile him up, only to reassure.

"I am not at all tempted," I promised him.

A blinding smile broke over his face.

To be sure I hammered this point in, I added, "Huxley, Ross, and Glenn are becoming amazing friends whom I'll always cherish. But you, Barrett, are home. That, my heart is very sure of."

This time, he kissed me, and I felt the tight grip he had on the back of my head like a brand of possession. I kissed him back, happy to do so, and hoped any insecurities he'd harbored died to ashes.

There were a few wolf whistles, but I ignored them. Reassuring my man took priority.

# 15

After staying up most of Saturday, I understandably slept in on Sunday.

Besides, sunlight. Ewww. I'd much rather stay cozied up with my werewolf boyfriend in our bed.

It was probably late afternoon, maybe edging toward early evening, when I felt him shift at my back and start nuzzling my neck—a sign he had woken up feeling frisky. You know, vampires were accused of neck-romancy, if you will, but I had a lot of hickies on my neck. Just saying, Barrett could give me a good run for my money in that department.

Still, if he was all ready to rumble, I was up for it. I smiled into my pillow before wiggling my ass against his groin.

"Mm," he growl-slash-groaned in delight. "So you are awake."

"I'm supposed to somehow sleep with you gnawing on my neck like that?" I teased.

"Speaking of gnawing, don't you want to feed from me while I'm fucking you?"

Barrett's hand slid around to tweak a nipple, the firm tug sending delicious sparks through my chest.

I'd fed from him once during sex and now the man was absolutely addicted. I had to admit, mixing blood and sex felt utterly natural to me, and it made our lovemaking tip over into hot jungle sex territory. Couldn't complain about that.

"I'd love—"

My damn phone rang.

It lay on my nightstand, vibrating a little with each ring,

and my eyes skewered it. How very dare you ring in this moment.

Barrett sighed and reached over me to fetch it. "Just answer."

But I don't want to. Fuck, guess I had to. I swiped *Accept* before I fully registered just who was calling. Why was Anthony calling? "Hey, what's up?"

Anthony sounded beyond distraught. *"Jesse, I need backup over here. The vampires are throwing their weight around, and we can't get them to back down."*

My lust instantly faded, and I already had my legs over the side of the bed before he could trot the full sentence out.

"Where are you?"

*"Northeast side of town, at Buffalo Park. We're up the trail a little bit. We were out here doing some ritual prep, and they just appeared. It's supposed to be public domain, but they're arguing they have priority and are trying to kick us out."*

Why the hell would they do that? Buffalo Park was mostly flat grassland with a small mountain on it, meant for hiking, mostly, or to do some fun outdoor picnics. There was nothing fancy about the place.

This reeked of a power play.

"On my way. Sit tight."

Barrett had already gotten out of bed and put his pants on.

Please note this made me very upset. I preferred my boyfriend sans pants, thank you very much. Still, I supposed if we were going to be in public, pants were a thing. Groaning, I followed suit, also finding clothes and pulling them on.

"I'm getting Glenn," Barrett informed me.

He was halfway out the bedroom door already, but I still called after him. "Why?"

"Because he's got more seniority as a vampire!" he called back.

Oh. Good thought, that. Actually, hadn't Ross mentioned something about Glenn normally mediating vampire clan conflicts? He might be the best choice to bring along regardless.

By the time I got downstairs—I had epic bedhead I had to deal with first, which I did expediently by ducking my head under the shower spray for a second—Barrett already had Glenn and Ross up to speed. Huxley, too. They were apparently awake and had been chatting in the kitchen.

I snagged keys from the keyring as I moved. "My car. It's the only one that can fit everyone. We'll talk strategy on the way."

All of us moved quickly, as we had to get there fast. From what Barrett's mentioned, boundary conflicts had a tendency to get ugly in a second flat, and no one wanted that to happen here. Buffalo Park was on the very edge of town, granted, so if something went wrong then it wasn't likely to be seen by humans. But it was also a weekend, so odds were good people could be there and just oblivious to the danger.

I didn't obey a single speed limit, my little car zooming along. It was a relief when the park came in sight, the bronze stagecoach and horses barring the road in a clear indicator. We paid the fee to enter the park quickly, then hightailed it farther along the gravel path. Fortunately, the sun was starting to set, so it wasn't high enough in the sky to cause ouchiness. Still, I'd rather not be out in this for very long.

I called Anthony the second I was free of the park entrance. "I'm here, how far along the path?"

*"We're up on the mountain trail, just above the base."*

I heard a male voice snarling something in a different language, but the tone was enough to go off. Unhappy vampire, check.

I whipped into the first parking spot I could find and quickly got out. I didn't see any humans in sight, so I started running. Of course, everyone else easily kept up with me.

Glenn ran at my side to speak into the phone. "Anthony, is it? I'm Glenn Ó Riagáin from Salem. Who's the vampires with you?"

*"I don't know, no one's saying names. There's four of them."*

Glenn glanced at me, but I shrugged ignorance. I'd not actually met any of the vampires here, except Blondie, the vampire who'd tried to take me out on first meeting, and Oscar, the pseudo head honcho vampire of this area.

"We'll be there in a minute." I ended the call, mostly because I wanted to throw a warning out without the vampires hearing me over the phone. "Look, I have to tell you, the vampires here are pretty volatile."

Barrett let out a growl, lips curling up to reveal his canines. He hadn't shifted, but I could tell he was damn close to doing so. "When I first met Jesse, I called the local vampire lieutenant, as I felt like it was the right thing to do. Oscar sent someone to my house, and the idiot tried to treat Jesse like a rogue. If not for my intervention, Jesse would have been killed on the spot."

Sadly the truth. I'd been too weak to fight him off then. I might still be too weak to really win an all-out fight. Scary thought, that.

In a very unnatural calm, Huxley said, "So it's fine for us to kill them if they get too rambunctious."

Glenn sighed, deeply. "Don't you start."

I eyed my sire over my shoulder. He did look mad enough to kill. Well, damn, my warning might have backfired. I hadn't meant to rile him up, only give him a heads-up.

Finally, we reached the mountain after what felt like years. With our speed, we were up the trail in seconds, and after rounding a curve in the trail, I finally spotted our quarry.

Anthony was easy to spot, wearing tennis shoes, shorts, and a white tank. With him were three other witches, or at least they smelled of magic, all wearing similar clothing and with backpacks in hand.

Facing off with them were four vampires, not a single one I knew. Barrett did, I think, as he let out a snarl of aggravation. Well, this didn't bode well.

Anthony turned to see who approached and lit up in relief. "Jesse."

"Yup, I'm here." For all the good I'd do. Really, this was Glenn's show, not mine. "Let's do introductions, shall we—"

A tall vampire with a very emo look to him—I mean, he was in full black, trench coat and all, despite the heat—stepped forward a little and snapped at me. "I won't listen to some barely turned child!"

Glenn stepped forward immediately, getting right into his face. His voice was a dark, throaty timbre that sent a shiver up my spine. "You'll listen to me."

Emo actually backed off half a step, notable fear in his eyes.

Could I be like Glenn when I grew up? Like, holy hell, I didn't know you could intimidate a person by just standing there. He radiated authority, like a king would. I could almost see the crown.

"I am Glenn Ó Riagáin of Clan Ó Riagáin. I am the Mediator."

The whatsit? I edged back a little and whispered to Ross, "What?"

"It's an official title," Ross murmured back. "Vampires have their own hierarchy, with designated titles for those they recognize. Glenn's done so many negotiations with the different clans, he was recently officially recognized as the Mediator. Even if you hadn't called us in, Jesse, he would have been obligated to step in and deal with this because of it."

Huh. News to me. It was awesome, though, because that meant he really did have the authority to shut them down.

Emo actually looked ready to piss his pants, so he recognized the title, at the very least. He fell back to whisper with his buddies, all of them now looking nervous as hell. Ha, served them right. Damn, this promised to be a good show. Where was the popcorn?

Look, I was petty, I'd never claimed otherwise.

Now that he had them cowed, Glenn turned and gave an eloquent bow to the witches. "I'm here to mediate. Who am I speaking with?"

"Uh, I'm Anthony." Anthony turned and gestured to the rest of the witches. "This is Mel, Ellis, Valerie, and Trish. None of us are high up in our coven. We'd need to call someone to negotiate with you."

"That's fine. I don't feel negotiations should take place here, either. Let's choose a neutral ground. Somewhere far from humans. We can choose a different location and reconvene in an hour."

In case things got explody? That was my suspicion.

Emo was already on the phone with someone—sounded like Oscar from the British accent—and relaying what was going on. Glenn strode right over to him and took the phone out of his hand before once again introducing himself and asking, "Negotiations on boundaries needs to happen today, where would you like to meet?"

Yup, I could see why he was the negotiator, all right. Man was smooth.

I couldn't help but ask Ross, "Does he use that voice on you in bed?"

Ross gave me a naughty little grin. "He does."

"I see why you married him."

"That was, admittedly, one reason."

I turned to ask Huxley, "Are we even necessary right now?"

"I feel superfluous," he admitted with a shrug. "I do want to see this play out, however. I do not want to live in fear of a boundary conflict hurting you."

He was such a protective father, seriously. I had to give him a quick hug, because while I still had to adjust to the idea of having a father figure in my life who gave two shits about me, it was nice to have one. He hugged me back, smiling, but his eyes were on Glenn. He really was paying close attention.

I was with him, though. I wanted to see this played out with my own eyes. Somehow, I felt like with Glenn in charge, the boundary issue that had plagued this area would get resolved today.

# 16

Their neutral meeting ground was a cemetery.

I wished I was making this up.

Everyone, for whatever reason, chose to meet at Citizens Cemetery.

I mean, it was kinda sorta not really in the middle of town? So thereby sort of neutral territory? I didn't know how to justify the decision, really, other than it was empty of people. Well, living people.

It was sort of charming, really, with the moonlit grass and the pine trees and all. So long as you watched where you were going to avoid tripping over tombstones, you were fine. Ross had us pack up a bunch of folding chairs for people to sit in, which was smart of him, as it wasn't like there were picnic tables or anything at our destination.

Still...of all places to choose...

As we unloaded from the car, Barrett also wrinkled his nose. "Why here?"

"See! I'm not the only one who thinks this is weird, right?"

Ross piped up as he slid out of the back seat. "Cemeteries are quiet, and the dead won't complain if we start making too much noise. Anyone who operates a cemetery ignores people that visit in groups, it's an unspoken understanding. So long as we don't break shit."

I turned and said accusingly, "It's your blood that influences you to think like this. A creature who walks the night likes being among the dead or something."

He lifted a pointed eyebrow at me. "Says the vampire."

Erk. I did forget somedays. Maybe living with wolves nonstop did it.

Anyway, we were here. Might as well get this over with. Hopefully Glenn could negotiate-slash-intimidate people into agreeing to some hard boundaries so territory conflicts stopped. That'd be lovely. I had priorities, after all. Barrett-shaped priorities.

We weren't the only ones to arrive, of course. The witches showed up in two full vans, while the vampires in three different SUVs. The whole clan was in unrelieved black, looking dark and mysterious. I took them in as they filed out of the vehicles, and some part of me became a little creeped out. Did they all dress in black to be more intimidating? Or was this just the norm for them? I hoped it wasn't the norm because it was kinda cultish. I felt very glad I hadn't ended up with them, as I had the feeling I would have left quickly.

Barrett took my hand as we walked into the cemetery. I liked holding hands with him, but we so rarely got the chance to do it. We hadn't had enough date nights, or chances to do date nights, really. I should take him on a date tonight, assuming this meeting let out anytime before midnight.

They chose a fairly empty spot under the trees, and people took advantage of the folding chairs, sitting promptly. Barrett tugged me down to sit next to him, which was fair. I was technically an alpha, too.

Vampires to my right looked at me like I'd dragged a wet, muddy dog into this for no good reason. Witches arrayed across from us, Glenn standing to my left, all of us forming one big circle. Honestly, I was a little unnerved smelling this much magic, being surrounded by this many witches, as it brought up bad memories.

Barrett must have sensed my unease, as he squeezed my hand firmly. I squeezed back, reassured. If they did try something, I had no doubt Barrett would throw down.

Ross manned a map and pencil, which he'd clipped to a poster board. That man thought of everything.

"All right, introductions first." Glenn put a hand to his own chest. "I'm the Mediator, Glenn Ó Riagáin. Witches, who is your leader?"

An elderly woman with greying hair at the temples stood. "I'm Vivian Griswold, head of the coven. I will speak for my coven."

"Thank you, noted. Vampires?"

Oscar grunted in acknowledgement. "I'm Oscar Deering, acting in my master's stead for this clan. I speak for the vampires."

"Thank you. Wolves?"

This must be some kind of formal etiquette thing since of course he knew Barrett. Still, my boyfriend didn't hesitate.

"Barrett Walker, alpha of my pack. I speak for the werewolves and my vampire."

Loved how he threw that in there, just tacking me on.

Oscar glowered at him but wisely didn't try and dispute it. I could feel Huxley standing at my shoulder, daring him to say a word. Huxley was still mad about the whole stabby thing.

"Thank you." Glenn took in a breath and on his exhale, he somehow seemed to fill the space. This man had charisma and prestige in spades. "Now, I understand that this being new territory, there's conflict on what should be neutral and who should have claims. Right now, let me get an idea of who is where. We'll go in order."

No one had any arguments, and they listed where their people were and such. Ross noted all this down on his map.

"Good, now, what should be neutral?"

Annnnd here we go. This was what had gathered us here today.

Oscar was the first to stir. "I do not think we agree on that. As previously discussed, the downtown public areas should be neutral. The main street, shopping centers, and government offices should also be neutral, of course, but I think the rest of Flagstaff should be divided with firm boundaries."

"Even if there's a park in your area, which we previously agreed would be accessible to all? So now you're saying we can't use public space because we'd have to cross through your territory to reach it?" Vivian challenged.

"Even then."

Ah, Oscar. You started out so well, sounding reasonable, only to reveal your douchiness in the end.

"By that logic, your vampires should not have been in Buffalo Park today," Glenn drawled, "considering the vampires claim the southeastern side of town. There's no way to reach that park without stepping into werewolf territory."

Oscar's mouth snapped shut and he glowered.

Ha, Glenn had him there.

Barrett stirred a little before speaking. "I do need a certain amount of desert for my wolves to run in. That said, I agree the city itself should be neutral space for us all."

"But some of our neighborhoods are in the middle of the city!" Vivian objected.

She did have a point. I mean, our subdivision was in the northeast section of town, so technically we were in "neutral" territory too.

Glenn held up a staying hand. "We can compromise this idea, I promise you. We had to do something similar in Salem, as Huxley can attest."

Huxley let out a sigh. "Yes, so you did, although god, I do not like to remember that argument. Three days of it."

Three days...yikes on bikes, do not tell me we were going to be sitting here for three days!

Save us, Glenn. You're our only hope.

While Glenn had spoken, Ross had been busy drawing. He turned the map to let his husband see, and Glenn gave him a soft, proud smile.

"Always so quick to anticipate me. Yes, that's fine."

He had Ross flip the map again so we could all see it as well.

I took a good look and then let out a low whistle. Oh-ho. Ross had drawn lines around each of our neighborhoods and then basically fanned them outward, beyond city limits, into the desert around us. The boundaries ended again when they hit another city limit, such as Kachina, to the south of us. It left each group a LOT of acreage, to say the least. Plenty of room for even two hundred wolves to stretch out in.

It also meant most of Flagstaff itself was neutral territory, with plenty of buffer space between each group.

Now, this I liked.

Oscar looked at it and grumbled. "Now, where are my vampires supposed to feed if we're assigned nothing but rocks and sand?"

"You can still hunt in town," Glenn said with some asperity. "No one's denying you a meal or some fun. I'm not telling the wolves or the witches they can't eat at restaurants, now am I?"

Oscar glowered some more.

Really, I felt like Oscar was just mad he wasn't in charge of the meeting. Such a petty soul, our Oscar.

Vivian lifted a hand, a wide smile on her face. "Personally, I like this division very much."

Next to me, Barrett gave a grunt. "Yes, it works out well for us, too."

We all turned and stared at Oscar. Oscar stared back. Oh, I could tell he was trying hard to think of an argument, but he couldn't quite vocalize anything without sounding like a whiny brat. Finally, he gave a sigh and looked deliberately elsewhere.

"Fine. It's fine."

Glenn ignored the attitude like a seasoned pro and whipped out an agreement form. "Then, everyone fill this out and sign it. I'll draw the lines in with a marker and have each of you sign on your territories as well. This all will be filed with the council, with copies given to each of you for reference."

Funny, he said reference, but I got this visual of him rolling the map up and smacking people in the head with it the second they started being obstinate. I believed he'd do it, too.

We all filled out paperwork, and Glenn did the redrawing with a thick black marker, which felt a little anticlimactic. I'd fully expected Oscar at least to start throwing hands at some point, but I had a feeling he didn't dare cross Glenn.

Once he'd collected the forms, Glenn gave us a polite smile. "Thank you all for coming. These boundaries begin immediately, so please inform your people."

Vivian immediately stood and came in closer. "Hold on, I want to take a picture of this with my phone to text everyone."

"Feel free," Glenn encouraged.

This was a good idea, so I immediately joined her, taking pictures and then putting them into the group chat.

The vampires were quick to leave and no one missed them. Huxley sidled up next to me, watching them pull out of the parking lot with a frown. "Promise me something."

I quirked a brow. "What?"

"If things go south—because I don't believe that one wants to obey the rules set today—then you need to come to me."

"Only if you're willing to take in two hundred werewolves because I won't be coming alone."

Ross's head snapped up and he went, "NO. No more werewolves!"

Eh?

Glenn laughed before correcting his husband, "Not for our clan, astór. Huxley would be the one dealing with them."

Ross glowered at Huxley, still not appeased. "Werewolves *find* trouble, do you understand what I'm saying? It can be a perfectly nice day, not a sign of trouble to be had, and they'll make trouble. They do ridiculous things like adopt every single dog out of a shelter and then go running around barking at random things all day. Do not encourage this!"

Huxley blinked at him, as if trying to wrap his head around this and failing. "They really adopted a whole pound of dogs? They can do that?"

"No one stopped them. And I tried, dammit," Ross whined.

It was a little concerning that Ross acted so scarred from this experience. Like, how bad had this actually gone down...?

Anyway, we were done now. Time to go home and celebrate.

Maybe, if I was lucky, I could get Barrett alone. We had interrupted sexy times to get back to.

A house full of wolves and guests would make it tricky, but I was both determined and clever. I was sure I could make it happen.

# Epilogue

*Two years later*

I sprawled on the couch, legs up, AirPods in while I spoke with Ross. I'd been calling to get an estimate of people's availability before setting an actual wedding date. Barrett had asked me to marry him this past weekend, and I'd been thrilled. It hadn't exactly been a surprise—he'd rented a cabin out in the woods for a romantic getaway and threatened the whole clan with death and dismemberment if anyone interrupted us, so I'd guessed he was up to something. Still, his proposal made me incredibly happy, and I'd immediately said yes.

Hence I was now in wedding prep mode, starting with trying to nail down a date.

Ross being one of the harder people to schedule, I'd called him right after speaking with Huxley.

"So, anytime in summer is out?"

"*Too many shenanigans happen in summer,*" Ross explained on a long sigh. "*November is generally good. September and October are all either prep for our haunted house or we're actually in the throes of it.*"

"November, eh? I'm okay with that. People don't generally do winter weddings, so the dates will be easier to schedule. Not to mention a little cheaper." I wrote a note to myself in my fancy three-ring binder. Marissa had given it to me and it said *Fairy Tale Pending* on the front.

Which was accurate. Maybe cheesy, but accurate.

"*How big of a venue do you need?*"

"Huge, man. Huge. And bring your dancing shoes, since dancing is huge in Cuban culture. I didn't even realize until I lived with them for several months how much they love to dance. Also, I don't know if Huxley has been keeping you up to date on what's been going on the past six months—"

"*Er, we don't actually talk all that much. Why?*"

"Well, we're basically becoming your clan, just a 2.0. It started with the witch coven hanging out with our pack, and then people started hooking up, and now I've got at least eight who are either married or engaged. Their coven and our pack are basically merged at this point."

Ross let out an incredulous sound. "*You're not serious.*"

"I'm not even exaggerating. Then, after that started happening, it was like this signal to the other supernats that we're chill or something, I don't know. We started finding these nomadic people who didn't have a home, and they'd ask for a place to stay for a few while they got their feet back under them, and then they just...didn't leave. I now have kobolds, house goblins, three dryads, and a whole flock of Thunderbirds—"

"*A whosawhatsit?*"

"Thunderbirds. Native mythology to North America, really. They're huge, wingspan is up to twenty feet. Our territory overlapped with one of theirs—they're more in the mountains—and they figured out we're chill to hang with, so they started participating in our moon runs, and now they're just in the pack. Apparently."

"*Barrett sure is easygoing about adopting the strays.*"

"Tell me about it. I thought it was my sexy charm and dynamic personality that had him taking me in, but apparently not. Anyway, the only ones still keeping their distance are the vampires. I think Oscar had been plotting something up until he realized we're now outnumbering him three to one, and all of a sudden, he's been quiet and low profile."

Ross chuckled, evilly amused. *"Good. That's how we like him."*

"Yup, for sure. Anyway, if you're good with November, I can run the date by Barrett—"

From outside the window, a lot of barking started up. Huh? That didn't sound right. Wolves had a sort of bark-growl sound, or a bark-howl. This had a totally different sound to it. This sounded like actual dogs, and there was quite the range, from something deep to very high-pitched.

I had the feeling something had gone awry. Suspicions, dark suspicions, coiled within my mind. Barrett and Luis had been talking about dogs the other day, saying something about "missing having a dog." I hadn't paid it much attention at the time.

That may have been my mistake.

I got up immediately, heading for the window. Through the glass, I got a visual of the situation. Three different SUVs had pulled up to the curb, and different members of my pack opened up doors with excited squeals before coaxing one dog after another out of the vehicles. All types, too— mutts, pitties, shepherds, terriers; I mean, it was a very wide assortment.

The dogs hopped down lightly and immediately sniffed everyone in sight before letting out happy barks.

*"Jesse? You still with me?"*

"Ross, I might have to let you go. For some reason, three SUVs loaded with dogs just pulled up in front of the house." Under my incredulous eyes, dogs just kept unloading from the cars. Was this a cartoon? Had they stuffed a million dogs into those three clown cars? "I swear, I think they emptied the pound."

From somewhere nearby I heard an excited, "PUPPIES!"

Aaannnd that had been Ria.

Ross laughed. He laughed because it was me having to deal with this and not him. Some friend he was. *"I definitely need to let you go. Good luck with that."*

"Yeah, thanks. I have a feeling I'm going to need it."

Thanks for reading *Adopt a Vampire*! This was originally a Patreon serial I released weekly in 2024, with story input from my patreons as I wrote it, and I had great fun. I've got more such serials ongoing, so if you want to read them now rather than having to wait six months to a year to read, check out my Patreon!

Want to know more about the two crossover appearances of Ross, Glenn, and Remi?

Looking for a funny (cracky, let's be honest), slice-of-life read? Poor Ross is up to his ears in supernatural problems, which is what happens when you're a PA for a supernatural clan. It's a good thing his vampire boss is so sexy. And gives him hazard pay. That helps too.

The Tribulations of Ross Young, Supernat PA

Assassins and thieves and hackers, oh my! The only thing is missing is—wait nope—badass child acquired!

How to Shield an Assassin

If you haven't tried my other M/F penname, Allie Brahms you should! It's urban fantasy/paranormal, so if that's your jam make sure to check it out.

What's the life of a ghost matchmaker like? Interesting to say the least. Waking up magically soul-bonded to the sexy demon slayer Zhen? -incoherent hand waving-

Tie Me Knot

And check out my Patreon for WIPS, short stories, and goodies!

*Books by AJ Sherwood*

Fated Mates
Fated Mates and When to Keep Them • Fated Mates and How to Woo
Them • Fated Mates and Where to Find Them

Gay 4 Renovations
Style of Love

Haelan
The Magic That Binds

Jon's Mysteries
Jon's Downright Ridiculous Shooting Case • Jon's Crazy Head-Boppin'
Mystery • Jon's Spooky Corpse Conundrum • Jon's Boom-Shaka-Laka
Problem • Jon and Mack's Terrifying Tree Troubles • Jon's Helter
Skelter Cold Case

Legends of Lobe den Herren
Fourth Point of Contact • Zone of Action • Starfire*

Mack's Marvelous Manifestations
Brandon's Very Merry Haunted Christmas • Mack's Perfectly Ghastly
Homecoming • Mack's Rousing Ghoulish Highland Adventure

R'iyah Family Archives
A Mage's Guide to Human Familiars • A Mage's Guide to Aussie Terrors
• A Mage's Guide to Wicky

Ross Young
The Tribulations of Ross Young, Supernat PA • LARPing • Common
Sense Deserts Again

The Sorcerer's Grimoire
A (Non) Comprehensive Guide to Sea Serpents • Dealing with
Mapinguari and Dogged Engineers

<u>Unholy Trifecta</u>
How to Shield an Assassin • How to Steal a Thief • How to Hack a
Hacker

<u>Villainy</u>
How I Stole the Princess's White Knight and Turned Him to Villainy
• How I Took the King on a Bone-a-fide Quest of Piracy, Piemu, and
Profit

The Coronation • How Tan Acquired an Apprentice

<u>Single Titles</u>
A Fae Coin Transported Me Into Another World and Now I'm the Gay
Holy Maiden • The Regressor King*

<u>Short Stories</u>
How to Keep an Author (Alive) • Marriage Contract • My Inherited
House Might Be Haunted • Adopt a Vampire

*Books by AJ Sherwood and Devon Vesper*

<u>Spellbound</u>
The Insanity of Reincarnated Mages and Amorous Vampires

*Books by AJ Sherwood and Jocelynn Drake*

<u>Scales 'n' Spells</u>
Origin • Breath • Blood • Embers • Wish (a Christmas novella)

<u>Wings 'n' Wands</u>
Dawn (a novella) • Ruins •Rise •Soar

# Author

AJ Sherwood (bigender, she/he pronouns) was born loving books. Her mother read her fairy tales and her father read her technical manuals, so was it any wonder she grew up thinking all books were wonderful? At five, she wrote and illustrated her first book.

At *mumbles age* she's written over a hundred books between multiple pennames, and has no intention of stopping before she climbs into a grave.

Right now, she lives in Michigan in a wonderful old Craftsman house with two dogs and four cats.

For more information about her books, to be notified when books are released, or get behind the scenes info about upcoming books, sign up or visit her at:

Newsletter or email: sherwoodnewsletter@ raconteurhouse.com
www.ajsherwood.com
FB: AJ's Gentlemen
Patreon (for WIPS, ARCs and goodies!)

Printed in Great Britain
by Amazon

62379229R00090